CHANGING
FILTHY
GARMENTS

CHANGING FILTHY GARMENTS

The Story of Mary Jacobs

LAMAR JOHNSON

XULON PRESS

Xulon Press
2301 Lucien Way #415
Maitland, FL 32751
407.339.4217
www.xulonpress.com

© 2022 by Lamar Johnson

All rights reserved solely by the author. The author guarantees all contents are original and do not infringe upon the legal rights of any other person or work. No part of this book may be reproduced in any form without the permission of the author.

Due to the changing nature of the Internet, if there are any web addresses, links, or URLs included in this manuscript, these may have been altered and may no longer be accessible. The views and opinions shared in this book belong solely to the author and do not necessarily reflect those of the publisher. The publisher therefore disclaims responsibility for the views or opinions expressed within the work.

Unless otherwise indicated, Scripture quotations taken from the New King James Version (NKJV). Copyright © 1982 by Thomas Nelson, Inc. Used by permission. All rights reserved.

Paperback ISBN-13: 978-1-66286-683-8
Ebook ISBN-13: 978-1-66286-684-5

Table of Contents

Chapter 1 1

Chapter 2 11

Chapter 3 17

Chapter 4 27

Chapter 5 39

Chapter 6 63

Chapter 7 73

Chapter 8 83

Chapter 9 87

CHAPTER 1

It was three o'clock in the morning and the loud ringing of the phone broke the silent morning air, startling Lois awake. "Hello?" she answered softly into the corded bedroom phone that rested on her nightstand.

"This is Quilla Mae, Lois." Another woman's soft voice responded through the speaker. "I apologize for calling you at this hour."

Quilla Mae was her best friend and fellow Sunday school teacher. If she was the calling, it was most certainly something important. Lois sat up, switched on her lamp, and looked at the small calendar on her nightstand, which read December 1980. Lois's heart fluttered with anxiety as she asked, "What's wrong?"

"It's about Mary…" Before Quilla Mae could finish her sentence, Lois dropped the phone, leapt to her feet, and dashed down the hall to check on her granddaughter, her beloved and only grandchild. Mary was sound asleep, snugly tucked under the covers of her bed.

After missing a beat, Lois's heart regained its natural rhythm, and she breathed a sigh of relief. She returned to her phone. "Mary is fine. She's asleep."

"Yes, I know. Please, let me explain." Quilla Mae, a true prophetess, took a deep breath before continuing. "I just had a vision. The Most High God appeared to me, and I saw Mary standing on a very tall mountain. She was speaking loudly and I saw women responding to her words. She was a beacon of light for those who were depressed, ashamed, abused, and outcasted."

Lois smiled as she listened. Her heart overflowed with gratitude and thanksgiving, quickly replacing her earlier feelings of fear and anxiety, as she could only anticipate what God had in store for Mary.

"I saw her win many souls for the kingdom of Yeshua," Quilla Mae continued. "Our Father in heaven was exalted. His grace clothed her, His light shone on her, and He was pleased."

"*Baruch Hashem!*" Lois exclaimed, He was faithful and just, and He deserved everything she said. She spoke blessings over Mary from the moment she was born, declaring that God would raise her up to do His will.

The two women prayed together until the sun came up, praying to God for protection, favor, grace, and mercy over their lives. After she hung up the phone, Lois wrote down every word she could remember from the call on a sheet of paper and placed it in an envelope with other words of prophecy from Yahweh kept safely in her nightstand drawer.

***

When the Lord revealed this vision to His servant, Mary was only eight years old. Amanda, Lois's daughter, had turned to a life of drugs, prostitution, and crime. Lois prayed that Mary would not be like her mother, the prodigal who refused to return home, and had taken Mary under her care after being granted full custody by the court. She had been the apple of her eye ever since.

Mary was an exuberant child who could frequently be seen laughing, smiling, and running. She also enjoyed going to Sunday school, church, and to Quilla Mae's large acre ranch, where she enjoyed riding horses, swimming, and playing tennis.

CHAPTER 1

Her outgoing personality continued into her adolescence as she developed into a young woman who was vivacious and inspiring. She was filled with boundless energy and her friends adored her radiant disposition. Everywhere she went, she was the life of the party.

Gorgeous skies, glorious sun sets, the pleasures of peace and security encamped around Mary. A period of tranquil glory and indescribable peace was her portion but even during the brightest of seasons, darkness has a way of rolling in, and one fateful morning when Mary was fourteen years old, her world would change forever...

Mary awoke groggy after a deep sleep. "What time is it?" she groaned as she rolled over and checked her alarm clock: 10:00 a.m. She was supposed to be at school two hours ago.

"Mom, I'm late! I overslept!" Mary yelled for her grandmother, the woman she referred to as mother, who was two doors down the hall. She quickly brushed her teeth, put on her clothes, and brushed her hair.

When she was all ready to go, she realized her mother didn't respond as she would have expected. She was usually up much earlier than Mary, the aroma of scrambled eggs, bagels, and freshly squeezed orange juice filling the house as she made breakfast... yet the wonderful aroma was not present and the house remained silent.

"Mom? Are you still sound asleep?" She called again, but her mother didn't answer. *She must be exhausted*, Mary thought as she went to her mother's bedroom and slowly turned the doorknob.

"Get up, mom! You must drive me to school!" Mary spoke loudly as she shook her mother, but still received no response. Mary took her ashen hand in hers... it felt so cold. She then rolled the old woman over and rested her hand on her peaceful looking face... it was stiff.

Mary released her mother's hand and stumbled back, tears streaming down her cheeks as she realized that her mother's spirit had left her body during the night.

CHANGING FILTHY GARMENTS

With trembling fingers, she dialed 911. She couldn't stop sobbing as she sat on the floor. This was the first time she had witnessed death so close… and she was all alone with no one to turn to for comfort. She had known people who had died and attended their funerals, but this was her grandmother, the woman she called mother and the most important person in her life.

What should I do now? Mary thought as she cried even more, but then she heard her grandmother's voice say in the back of her mind, "The saints of God don't die; they go on to be in the bosom of the Father." Ironically, beside her bed was her Bible, which was opened to 2 Corinthians 5:8. *We are confident, yes, well pleased rather to be absent from the body and present with the Lord.*

Once the ambulance arrived, the paramedics confirmed Lois's death. The police and social workers stayed with Mary at her house until her biological mother arrived. Amanda arrived hours later in an old, dented, rusted car driven by a man. He appeared irritated as his cold black eyes fixed on Mary. Amanda stepped out of the passenger's side door, her skirt barley covering her vulva, and affixed the crooked wig on her head. She nearly fell as she approached the social worker, blaming her dirty, scuffed up high heels. She squinted at the social worker and her daughter, her vision blurred by the drugs and alcohol.

The exasperated social workers and police relinquished their responsibility to Amanda after a lengthy conversation that finally confirmed that she was Mary's mother. Mary climbed into the back seat of the filthy car, which was littered with beer cans, liquor bottles, pill bottles, cigar wrappers, and needles.

"Mary, this is my boyfriend Talmai. Talmai, this is my daughter," she said casually as she burped and sat back in the passenger seat. Amanda had barely shut the car door when her eyes rolled to the back of her head and she passed out. Through the review mirror, Talmai narrowed his eyes at Mary, his eyes cunning and sinister. She said hello quietly and quickly averted her gaze from

CHAPTER 1

the tattoos on his face. She already missed her grandmother and could sense the darkness that both of the people in the car possessed.

The body of Christ filled the sanctuary at Lois's memorial service. The house of worship was packed as the entire town of Baxley, Georgia came to pay their respects to the divine woman. No one said anything negative as her friends and colleagues came to witness her humility and meekness as a pillar of strength for her community. One of God's ambassadors had entered His eternal glory and rest, and the saints of God shouted and danced in a sorrowful, yet joyful celebration. Following the benediction, everyone drove to the burial site where the coffin was placed in the ground and Mary and Quilla Mae said their final farewell.

Mary moved in with Quilla Mae on her sprawling ranch. She loved riding horses, swimming, playing tennis, and running around the track Quilla Mae had paved for her. The fresh air was beneficial to Mary, and she spent the majority of her time outside as did Quilla Mae. She went to scripture study and worship service on a regular basis, just like her mother always had. Quilla Mae, like her mother, became her spiritual mentor and taught her God's Word, and the two often shared stories about Lois late into the night. Despite the fact that Mary missed her mother and Quilla Mae missed her best friend, the two assisted each other in healing.

***

Months passed as Mary continued to heal from the loss of her mother. She was slowly becoming happier and healthier again as her broken heart continued to mend. She had a sturdy foundation as school and life on the ranch with Quilla Mae was good, but Amanda was growing increasingly resentful and jealous as she heard the scoffs of the people of Baxley judging her for not raising her own child.

Talmai was no exception. His raucous personality led the chorus of a lifelong criminal with extensive knowledge of schemes and scams. He convinced Amanda that they were losing money by not housing Mary. The assistance provided by food and government housing would be invaluable, so they devised a strategy to obtain welfare through Mary.

Unfortunately, Quilla Mae was not her legal guardian and there was no blood relation, and while Lois would have preferred Mary to remain with Quilla Mae, she did not have a will. Quilla Mae fought valiantly, hiring the best lawyer in Baxley, but it was all for naught. The biological mother had a right to her daughter and the courts could do nothing about it.

When Mary got home from school one day, Quilla Mae told her about the court's decision. Mary was heartbroken. She begged Quilla Mae to let her stay, but there was nothing Quilla Mae could do.

"There has to be something!" Tears streamed from Mary's eyes, her voice cracked with fear and pain as she cried on her knees.

Quilla Mae wiped her tears as she helped Mary to her feet. "I'll go back to the court and keep fighting for you," she said, hugging her even tighter.

Amanda sat in the car with Talmai, both of them laughing at the "overly sentimental" encounter before them. At Talmai's urging, Amanda exited the vehicle and demanded that Mary retrieve her belongings.

Quilla Mae and Mary remained in their sorrowful embrace, refusing to sperate right away. When they finally did part, Quilla Mae reaffirmed what she had always told her, "God favors you. He has a strategy for you. He has a plan for you."

Mary went upstairs to gather her belongings, kissed her spiritual mother good-bye, then got into the car with Amanda and Talmai.

CHAPTER 1

***

Mary's world began to darken from that day forward. Even though Talmai lived with them, Amanda brought man after man into their trailer home. Mary witnessed cocaine, crack, meth, and alcoholism abuse daily as well as verbal and physical abuse. The only relief she received was when she went to see Quilla Mae on the ranch.

During these visits, Quilla Mae would pray for her, speak power and strength into her, believe in her, and listen to her. "One day God will use you for His glory. He will make your name great, and through you, He will bring many people into His kingdom," she said.

As she ran sprints and rode horses in her sanctuary, Mary imagined how God would accomplish this. The faster she ran, the more tranquil she felt, as if she could run away from all of her problems.

Mary tried out for the school track team at the urging of Quilla Mae. She not only made the team, but quickly became the team captain as she was not only the fastest on the team, but the fastest in the county. When Mary ran track, she was whole and healthy, and she could lift her head high! It filled the void left by her mother's death with Amanda's abysmal home life.

With all of the accolades and awards she received for her achievements on the track, she wondered if this was how God would use her. Perhaps this was how she would honor God, her mother Lois, and her spiritual mentor. The anticipation of becoming a gold medalist, having her face on cereal boxes, endorsement deals, and commercials made her practice harder and desire it more and more.

It wasn't long before her name was acclaimed, and she began receiving full-ride offers from Division I schools for her track success. This only strengthened her conviction that God would make her famous through track. She saw His favor on her through her skills on the track, and she knew this would be the door that would open many more. She imagined it at school, at practice, and when she lay in her bed, and the fortune and fame she would receive made her giddy.

Quilla Mae, a wise woman of God, would always warn her, "I don't know how He's going to use you, but He promised He would. God is not a man to lie nor a son of man to repent. He had said it, and He will make good on it."

Mary would nod reassuringly, but it was so obvious to her that God was going to do His plans for her through track. So, she continued to work on her craft, believing it was her destiny.

Life was good as things began falling into place and she had a goal to achieve. Even though she technically lived with Amanda on paper, Mary spent the majority of her time at the ranch where she did her homework, ate dinner, and slept on a regular basis. Mary was summoned to come home only when Amanda needed to prove the child's whereabouts for governmental workers to continued receiving living, food, and other social assistance. This usually only lasted a week before Mary could resume her peaceful life back with Quilla Mae.

One day as she checked the ranch mailbox, she was overwhelmed with more Division I offers, but this day was filled with the one she had coveted. She dashed inside to show her spiritual mentor.

"I got! I got!" Mary screamed at the top of her lungs, overjoyed. Quilla Mae was so startled that she dashed downstairs to investigate. "It's arrived! It's finally here! It's from the University of Los Angeles!" Mary shook with anticipation as she hugged Quilla Mae. Quilla Mae hugged her back as they laughed together.

Mary loved California because of the influence of TV shows, movies, and music. She was ready to sign the acceptance letter from Coach Len Walker right then and there. Los Angeles was the place to be what movie stars, musicians, the ocean, the weather, and the culture! Before Mary

CHAPTER 1

committed to the university, Quilla Mae advised her that they should first meet Coach Walker for dinner.

Three weeks after the request to meet, the coach flew into Savannah and drove to Baxley to have dinner at Quilla Mae's ranch. He was driven, charismatic, and convincing as he bragged about the numerous champions that his teams had produced over the years. He was obsessed with winning, and that was all he spoke about.

Mary hung onto every word he said because she knew what it took to be a winner: focus, drive, and hard work. She wanted to be a part of a winning tradition, and this would help her get closer to having her name in the spotlight and establish herself in the sports industry.

While Mary adored the coach, Quilla Mae thought he was fickle. She refrained from being obsequious out of respect for Mary, but she could tell Mary was just another athlete to him as they only talked about how he could improve her time, techniques, and wins. He never once inquired about Mary as a person, her story, her likes and dislikes, only addressing her as if she were an object. She could see his only concerns were what Mary could do for his team, his reputation, and the zeros in his paycheck when the team won all the championships.

Mary was eager to sign, but she listened to Quilla Mae when she suggested that she take a few days to pray about it.

After Coach Walker's visit, Mary still hadn't received the blessing from her spiritual mentor. The days continued to fly by, and Mary began to worry that if she didn't sign soon, Coach Walker may rescind the offer letter. Still, Quilla Mae expressed her dissatisfaction with the decision and asked the Lord for guidance.

Quilla Mae awoke at twilight, as was her custom, and put on her tallit before entering the spacious room she had dedicated to her God. She knelt on her knees and raised her hands to Jehovah, the Creator of heaven and Earth. She started reciting the Lord's Prayer. "My Father in heaven, hallowed be Your name. Your kingdom come, Your will be done on Earth as it is in heaven."

She had barely uttered the final word of her prayer when she suddenly heard the Lord speak to her.

"*Incline your ear to hear. I have appointed Mary as a watchman to a people who have been accosted, shamed, brokenhearted, and assaulted. I will bless her, and she will bless others. The enemy will flood in, but I will raise a standard against him. His disgraceful actions will be used to My glory. She will overcome by My blood and the word of her testimony. Warn her not to harden her heart. The devil's foothold will be destroyed. I have not abandoned her.*"

The Lord commanded Quilla Mae to pray for Mary night and day. Quilla Mae told Mary everything God had said, but Mary didn't want to hear any of it; she just wanted a yes! She was frustrated because she needed an answer. Coach Walker didn't care about her being the fastest in the region and the state for he had plenty of girls to pick from. She was irritated and tremulous not only because time was running out, but also because Amanda had called her. It was time to renew her food assistance and housing.

CHAPTER 2

Nothing had changed under Amanda's roof as alcoholism, drug use, and her mother prostituting herself for Talmai continued. When the cursing and verbal and physical abuse became too much for her, Mary locked herself in her room. She couldn't wait to get away from the darkness that drew her in; she was ready to return to peace, order, and harmony.

She was starving after a long day of practicing, so she opened the cabinets and found no food. *There is never any food here*, Mary thought to herself as her mother and Talmai would sell all of the government assistance they received to buy drugs and alcohol. As she went through each cabinet, she made her way to the refrigerator, thought she did not expect different results. She opened the refrigerator and found beer, old ketchup and mustard bottles, and a pot of greenish pasta that appeared to be a month old.

Bent over, she continued to navigate the bleak appearance of the refrigerator when Talmai crept up behind her and began to admire her well-built physique. The constant training had developed Mary's body into being firm and attractive. She was seventeen, but her stature was that of a mature young woman.

Full of cocaine, he lusted after her voluptuous body and perfectly shaped buttocks. Over six feet tall and with a large and muscular build, Talmai approached her like a leopard stalking his prey. Still, unaware of his presence, Mary hoped for something to fill her now noisy stomach.

Talmai became more aroused by her wide hips, the predator fondled himself before he pounced on her like a hyena, ripping her shirt and bra off and staring at her plump breasts.

Mary couldn't get away. He had a fist full of her hair in one hand while his free arm was wrapped around her waist. She screamed, but there was no one who could hear her. He ripped the button from her pants and inserted his thigh between hers. Her five-foot-nine, 145 pound frame was no match for his strength. After ripping off her shirt and pants, he used his strong hands to pin her wrists to her sides.

He forced himself inside her. The physical pain and violation struck Mary like an ice pick through the heart. With each stroke, she died inside.

Why… Mary was in shock as her thoughts began to race. *I am chosen by God! He has a plan for my life! I sing His praises wherever I go! How can this be happening?! God, why are You letting this happen?!*

After he finished, Talmai wrapped his fingers around her neck. "If you tell anyone, I'll kill you and your mother," he threatened. "I've been to prison many times before and don't mind going back." He placed his pants back on and left Mary shaking and bleeding on the floor. Her purity had been stolen in a single heinous act. She had dreamed of a blissful marriage one day with her husband in an undefiled bed in holy matrimony, a blood covenant of light, but now it was shattered in darkness.

She cried for what seemed like hours on the floor until she ran out of tears. She finally managed to push herself to her feet, still in shock from the horrific assault, and limped her way to the bathroom. She slowly walked into the shower, hoping to scrub away the hurt, pain, and shame, but no matter how hard she washed her skin, she couldn't feel clean. She finally gave up and laid across her bed, the seed of rage, fury, and hypersexualism germinating in her heart.

CHAPTER 2

When Amanda returned from getting more drugs, she found Mary motionless across the bed, her face solemn from the many tears she had shed. "What's wrong?" Amanda asked.

Resentment seeds began to sprout within Mary's heart at the sound of her mother's voice. Part of this was her fault. Why did she insist she return to this God-forsaken place? She wanted to lash out at her, but when Talmai entered the bedroom, Mary looked at him with terror, knowing he was a man of his word and would kill them both, so she answered, "Nothing," unwilling to reveal his satanic secret. Amanda didn't investigate any further as she and the rapist went back to their room and smoked meth.

Mary stayed in her room the rest of the day. Tears streamed down her cheeks as her mind replayed the image of her being raped again and again. *How could something like this happen to me? What happened to God? Where is His shield? Why didn't Quilla Mae fight harder for me in court? Why did God take my mother? Why does this… woman have me?* The enemy planted seeds of indignation, bitterness, and renunciation for God inside of her head and heart.

After receiving another threat from Talmai the next day, Mary dressed and gathered her belongings for school. She remained a silent wreck in class, her heart fluttering between sorrow and rage. Her classmates and teachers all noticed the difference as she was always known for her amiable personality, always outgoing, warm, and jovial. The rape and rapist cast a deep web of darkness over her… There was no longer any humor, joy, or light shining through her.

Mary didn't talk to her friends for weeks and avoided all contact with Quilla Mae. During this time, the perverse, ungodly man raped her whenever he pleased. She was frustrated and crushed. Instead of a man and his father going into the same girl as Amos 2:7 said, her situation was flipped. It was one man who entered both the mother and the daughter.

She despised herself and her situation. She went from being an honor student to barely passing. People who partied and drank became her friends. Having sex out of wedlock was unthinkable before, but now boys in her class knew her. She was unrecognizable, in total opposition to the person she was becoming.

As announcement week approached, all student athletes were required to make their decision on what college to attend. Quilla Mae received instruction from the Lord on what Mary should do, but after several attempts of trying to contact the young woman, she was unable to relay the message for Mary had cut off all communication with her. It was of no consequence to Mary, though. She was hell-bent on attending the University of Los Angeles and no longer valued God, her spiritual mentor's prophecies, or her opinions.

After numerous failed attempts to see Mary, Quilla Mae refused to be denied any longer. She went to Amanda's trailer home one day after school and refused to leave as she continuously knocked on the door. The constant knocking irritated Mary, who looked out the window of the dilapidated trailer before she pushed open the door. Quilla Mae was overjoyed to see her mentee and spiritual daughter, but when she reached out to hug her, Mary drew away, choosing to cross her arms and lean against the trailer's doorframe.

Quilla Mae was hurt by Mary's action, but did not allow it to stop her from speaking to her. "How are you doing, dear? I've been so concerned. I've tried calling you and have stopped by several times. Why haven't you come to see me?"

"I'm fine. Focusing on running and getting out of here," Mary replied bitterly.

"That is why I am here. When I was praying in my heavenly language for you in my study, the Lord spoke to me and said, 'Warn Mary that accepting the scholarship to the school in Los Angeles will result in many hardships and self-inflicted burdens.'"

Her words enraged Mary. "I'm not listening to you anymore! I'm no longer listening to God, either!" she screamed angrily at the woman of God. "How can a loving God allow someone to hurt me?! What happened to His divine protection? Why did He let my true mother die and

CHAPTER 2

abandon me? I need her here! I wouldn't be here if she was here! What made Him take her away from me? Why has He abandoned me?!" Mary's anger quickly changed to sorrow as she began to weep, her spirit and soul anguishing in pain and agony.

Mary's heart had become hardened toward God and the people of God. Quilla Mae rushed forward and embraced Mary, but the tormented track star was unresponsive. Mary began to struggle after a few moments, trying to break free, but her mentor clung to her, refusing to let her out of her loving arms. Finally, Mary wrapped her arms around her spiritual mentor, hugging her back.

"I miss my mom! I don't want to be here anymore!" Mary cried out of her spirit. While she sobbed, the silhouette of the predator appeared, standing behind Mary.

Mary abruptly ceased speaking and lowered her head, quickly retracting from Quilla Mae's embrace and stepping back into the trailer.

"Mary, what's wrong?" As Quilla Mae pressed her to speak, she noticed the terrified expression Mary gave to Talmai.

"Nothing is wrong," Mary answered softly, lying in fear to Quilla Mae, but the woman of God was already certain about what was going on.

She asked Mary if she wanted to go to the police station, but she quickly declined. When she asked if she wanted to come live with her, the molester looked at Mary with a still fury, his eyes seeming to pierce through her. Mary immediately said "no" when she imagined the impending punishment.

The five-foot-two-inch powerful woman of God stepped into the trailer, approached the six-foot-four creep, and prayed aloud to her Father while looking at him. "Father, You said in Your Word in Proverbs 11:21 'the wicked will not go unpunished, but the posterity of the righteous will be delivered.' I call for Mary to be delivered from this vile man. Bring judgment on this infidel."

Talmai scoffed, but the woman of God persisted, her words pierced the force field of darkness every time the world of light was spoken. "Psalm 81:14 says, 'I would soon subdue their enemies and turn My hand against their adversaries.' Abba, this man is a foe; deal with him in accordance with Your Word and his actions.

"Heavenly Father, You said in Your Word that You will defeat Your people's enemies and fight their battles. Holy Spirit, I command a war angel to come and draw a sword and stretch it out over this man in accordance with 1 Chronicles 21:16.

"Spirit of the Living God, I agree with you in Micah 5:9. 'Your hand shall be lifted up against your adversaries, and all your enemies will be cut off.' Cut off this loathsome covenant breaker in the name of Jesus the Christ. Deliver her from the clutches of her oppressor in the name above all names, Yeshua."

The sword infiltrated the darkness around Talmai. The commander of heaven's army immediately dispatched a war angel. Armed with his sword, he held it over the invader's head. The war angel rendered Talmai impotent, his light breaking through the vast darkness accomplishing verdict. He never violated Mary or entered another woman again after that, and was taken to prison once more for his crimes.

Quilla Mae commanded Mary to retrieve all of her belongings and took her to the ranch. She was able to finish her senior year without being attacked, but the evil one's fiery darts had still penetrated Mary's soul, planting the seed of rebellion in her heart. A constant rage and fury would be its offspring.

CHAPTER 3

Announcement day arrived, and she chose the University of Los Angeles in direct defiance of God. She finished her high school career without much academic success, but she remained the fastest runner in the state of Georgia.

Her college dormmates and roommate were polite and considerate. Her classes were challenging, but as a highly valued student athlete, she was greatly assisted by her professors. She liked the dryness of the West Coast climate as the temperature was always pleasant. She didn't have to deal with the humidity of an East Coast summer, and there was no winter, so she could work on perfecting her craft all year.

Adjusting to the fast pace of life in Los Angeles was difficult. When she went out, there were so many people moving so fast because the effects of being raped had imprisoned her into being hypervigilant, reserved, and overly cautious. She was no longer able to trust anyone, and she frequently had to battle suicidal thoughts. She walked in a constant black cloud of depression that followed her wherever she went.

Her freshman and sophomore years were lonely, so she focused all of her attention and concentration on running, which was the only thing that kept her alive. It was the only time she didn't consider killing herself... or killing Talmai. On the track, she was free to run, and she ran until every tendon, ligament, and muscle in her body was exhausted, but like many high school athletes, she discovered the hard way that she was no longer the best. Teammates as well as other athletes from opposing teams were significantly faster, which broke her confidence and caused her to fall out of Coach Walker's favor.

She was the weakest link on the relay team in sprints and in hurdles. Coach Walker chastised her after every loss in competitions and practice. "You are no good to me if you can't win. I recruited you here to win. I gave you a scholarship because I thought you were a winner."

The constant barrage of verbal insults shattered her already frail spirit. Mary feared her scholarship would be revoked, and the dark cloud of depression that hung over her grew heavier as her junior year progressed. She wondered and considered returning to Baxley.

One day after yet another practice where Mary was humiliated in front of the team, she had had enough and stormed up to Coach Walker, profanity on the tip of her tongue. She knew she would lose her scholarship, but she didn't care. She couldn't take it any longer and was ready to hurl expletives when she was stopped by Athaliah.

Athaliah was the only person Mary spoke with on the team and was also her best friend, the only one she loved and trusted. Everyone adored Athaliah as she was friendly and affectionate. She grabbed Mary before she could get any closer to Coach Walker.

"Don't do this, Mary," she said in a low voice. "You'll lose your scholarship, you won't be able to pay for school, and you won't graduate."

"I don't care. Let me go."

"You will care because if you don't graduate, you're going to end up as one of three types of people."

"Only three? And what might those three be?"

"Those who can count and those who can't."

CHAPTER 3

Mary couldn't help but laugh at her friend's bad joke. Athaliah had a way of incorporating jokes directly into a conversation and her witty sense of humor always seemed to sooth her. She was the only person on campus who could make her smile and make her feel good about herself.

She was also the only person who knew her story. Athaliah had been raped by her mother's boyfriend, too, but instead of becoming isolated, angry, depressed, and enraged, she used her scars to wreak revenge on mankind through sexual exploitation.

Since the time of her rape, she used her untamed passions to be sexually indiscriminate against the male gender. Instead of being the prey, she became the predator.

Mary admired Athaliah's perceived liberation. She yearned for power after being raped, and the mirage of power that Athaliah displayed enticed her. They began to party more together, and she saw Athaliah give herself to men and women, using her sexuality as a tool to badger anyone she found appealing.

Watching Athaliah flaunt her licentiousness made Mary reconsider her position on sexuality. Perhaps this could be the way to lift the dark cloud that hovered over her. Why should she be loyal to God and His teachings on fornication if her virginity had already been stolen? He'd broken His divine promise to protect her, and now all cards were on the table.

Her lust grew stronger as she attended more parties. The more she saw sexual acts performed, the more she craved to be touched, and the more Athaliah was the center of attention, the more she craved that same attention.

All that she had been taught in the scriptures by her mother and spiritual mentor she purposefully rejected absolving herself from 1 Timothy 4:2. *Speaking lies in hypocrisy, having their own conscience seared with a hot iron.*

She flaunted her hourglass figure, plump breast, and thick thighs, especially off campus where sexual intercourse was plentiful. Older distinguished men with money and resources enjoyed her the most and she enjoyed weaponizing her sexuality for profit. She reasoned with herself that what she was doing was not wrong for men had been paying women for their "services" for years.

She became a high-end prostitute, and her world changed quickly. Celebrities and stars began requesting her services, and she was always at affluent parties and clubs, making more money than she had ever seen or dreamed of. It came quickly and easily, and she was overwhelmed by all of the requests.

When Coach Walker arrived at her large and opulent apartment to confront her about the missed practices and competitions, she laughed in his face and hurled wads of cash at him. "I don't need your scholarship!" she yelled before she slammed the door in his face.

Athaliah stayed in the same high-rise and they hung out all the time; there was never a dull moment. Athaliah was a true friend and confidant, and Mary trusted her more than anyone else.

Mary's name was being whispered more and more until her prostitution was no longer a secret. By her senior year in college, everyone on campus and in Los Angeles knew who she was. With fame came more opportunity for the world's riches, and she answered at every turn.

She did manage to graduate college with a bachelor's degree in communications, partly because she slept with the male professors and bribed other faculty members. Rather than wanting a job, Mary wanted power and fame, and she rejected the conscience of good will and morality when Quilla Mae called. Quilla Mae warned her to follow God's way, but this accretion was meet with ridicule Mary wanted to be ornated and celebrated.

She had tasted the forbidden fruit and was hooked; she desired the world and all of its glory. Rather than rejecting Satan and the temptations he dangled before her as Jesus had in Matthew 4:8, she desired and went after more.

CHAPTER 3

She drove luxury sports cars and lived in a downtown condo. She wore the latest high-end fashion, ate at the best restaurants, and partied with celebrities. She was living the life she desired, despite the scars and pain she had suffered in Baxley.

Her voluptuous, flawless body and soft, smooth skin enticed men, and she was eventually contacted by Ron Steele, a company executive from Two-Lip Entertainment, a company that owned several pornographic production companies and magazines.

"I can turn you into a star, Ms. Jacobs," Ron said. "I can make you the face of the industry. What you're making now are pennies compared to what you can make. With Two-Lip, every man in America will know your name." What Mary heard was music to her ears. Assiduous living was for losers; a life of effulgent living was for her.

Ron handed over a contract worth more than $500,000.00 at the corporate headquarters. Mary saw the zeros and immediately signed the contract without reading the fine print. She was told she would start in a few weeks, but first, Ron wanted to meet at a hotel to sample the goods. Mary, no stranger to the business, forced him to pay. When they were done, he left her payment on the table. Mary called Athaliah, and the two celebrated with champagne and lines of cocaine.

As they celebrated, Mary gazed out of the highest and most expensive skyscraper in the city, thinking of the acclaim she would receive. Her name would be known, just as Quilla Mae had predicted.

The twenty-two-year-old from Baxley began her pornography career. Her first day on the job, everyone expected her to be shy toward the camera and her coworkers, but she was neither shy nor nervous. She excelled in front of the camera and did not require much coaching as most of her scenes were correct on the first take.

Her first year was fantastic. Both male and female partners enjoyed working with her for she was energetic, professional, and she loved what she did. As Ron promised her, she became the industry's number one woman. Anyone who watched pornography knew who she was. People would approach her on the street and send fan mail to the studio where she worked.

For eight years she ruled the porn industry. She had wealth, fame, and the splendor of the world. She had friends, and she was celebrated everywhere she went.

During this time, she married a coworker, Billy Hunter. Athaliah served as her maid of honor. She lived the life of the business–drinking, drugs, and overspending. Mary Jacobs Hunter had mansions on both coasts, exotic cars, and vacation homes around the world. She partied and dined with movie stars, athletes, and celebrities.

During the spring of her ninth year, Mary took a day off from her reign, tired of the constant work and endless partying. She fell into a deep sleep while in bed watching TV and began to dream.

In her dream, she saw herself with no makeup, no jewelry, no designer clothes, no cars, and no homes; the very absence of her glamorous and flamboyant lifestyle. She was penniless, reduced to the status of a pauper, her face and body no longer desired; she was rejected, sorrowful, and bereaved. People pointed and laughed as she walked down the street. Once gawked at, waved to, and embraced, she was now vilified and scorned. Once a loved person now cursed and shamed. Her material possessions had been abandoned, her mansion demolished. She ran to Ron's arms, but he did not recognize her. She called for her husband Billy, but he did not respond.

She awoke in a cold sweat, shivering with terror. The dream was so vivid and real that she looked around and realized she was still in her mansion. Her expensive jewelry remained perfectly safe on the dresser and her Egyptian sheets still adorned her body, but it was so intense and clear that it distressed her greatly.

Mary told Billy about the dream when he got home from work. "Yeah, that sounds crazy," he said, unconcerned. "Dreams and visions are not real. When people tell me about their dreams, I feel they are concocted. You're fine, I'm fine, everybody's fine."

CHAPTER 3

Mary offered no resistance. When challenged, Billy could be intimidating and invective, but she had been taught that God sometimes used dreams as warnings to prepare people, and she knew in her heart that this dream meant something.

Mary had another strange dream after the two had retired for the night. The wind blew her upward toward the heavens, and lightning flashed around her, casting a bright light in her face. She stood on a golden stage with a microphone in her hand, encouraging women who were remorseful and willing to repent that if they confessed their sins and accepted Yeshua's atonement on the cross, they would not be condemned.

Smiling while sleeping, an indescribable and immense warmth washed over her, unlike anything she'd ever felt before. The light was blinding, radiant, and flowing through her. It was pure and unconditional, and the voice said emphatically, "*I will use you for My glory.*" She awoke from her dream when she heard the alarm clock.

"Wake up!" Mary yelled as she frantically pushed and shook her husband beside her.

"Let me guess… the dream, right?" Billy responded groggily and sarcastically.

"No, this time was different!" Mary then went on to describe her dream.

"That's fantastic, Mary. I hope your dream comes true," Billy said before he got up to get dressed, dismissing the dream once more; however, Mary lay in bed recalling her mother telling her the story of Joseph and Pharaoh in Genesis 41:32. *And the dream was repeated to Pharaoh twice because the thing is established by God, and God will bring it to pass shortly.*

Ron called her to the office the following day. She was informed that her contract would not be renewed. The owner wanted a new younger star to be the face of his empire, and her weight gain, drug use, and alcohol abuse all played a role in his decision. Mary begged him to reconsider, swearing to him that she would lose weight and never use drugs or drink again, but the decision was final, and she could expect her final payment within the next week.

CHANGING FILTHY GARMENTS

Devastated and demoralized, Mary drove over to Athaliah's house to seek comfort and reassurance that only a friend could provide. When Mary arrived at her condo, she noticed a Porsche similar to hers. When she looked at the license plate number, she realized it was Billy's car. She made her way to Athaliah's door and knocked.

"Just a second!" Athaliah called from behind the door, unsure of who was on the other side. Mary's heart sank when Athaliah opened the door. She stood with only her bra and panties… while Billy stood naked behind her. All three were stunned and silent.

Mary's knees almost gave way as she felt her chest being ripped open with someone's bare hands. When Billy approached, she shoved him and ran to her car, wondering how long this had been going on and finally understand why he had had so many "late-night meetings" at work. She planned to burn everything he had.

She vomited as soon as she stepped out of her car on her driveway. Weary and weak after the contents of her stomach were emptied, she sat on the hood of her car, tears streaming down her cheeks, having never felt so lost or alone in her life.

She had lost her job and her husband in one day, so to relieve the pain in her heart and soul, she snorted cocaine and drank until she was unconscious. She did this for weeks as no adult film content providers would open their doors to her.

Mary wanted it to be over. She wanted to feel nothing. Alcohol, cocaine, and pills were the cure to numbness, and she hoped the drugs would end her life, but God would not let her die.

For months, no matter how much cocaine she sniffed, how much alcohol she drank, or how many sleeping pills she took, she couldn't die by overdose. Desperate, she bought a .38 Special. Fearful of death, but unwilling to live, she loaded one bullet into the chamber and played Russian roulette. She pointed the gun at her own head.

Click!

CHAPTER 3

She rolled the chamber again, then raised the gun to her head.

Click!

She placed the gun to her head for the third time, her right index finger on the trigger, ready to squeeze. Her soul was grievous, her body shook uncontrollably as she tried to breathe through her sobs.

There was suddenly a knock at her motel door. Still at war with herself, yet curious of her mysterious visitor, she answered the door. Her neighbor stood before her. He hadn't seen her out in several days and was there to offer her a sandwich.

He immediately noticed the gun still in her right hand as soon as she opened the door. "Give me the gun," he said calmly, holding his hands out. Mary shook her head, returning the barrel to her temple. When she closed her eyes, the man was quick enough to grab her wrist and point the gun up.

They were both terrified as the bullet passed through the ceiling. He took possession of the gun and called the cops. They took her to the hospital after she made a statement and admitted her to the psychiatric ward. She was then transferred to a rehabilitation center specializing in depression and drug addiction.

The withdrawal from drugs and alcoholism and being reduced to poverty and loneliness brought back horrid memories of being raped… and of the many foolish decisions she had made in the years to follow. It made the first months of rehab extremely difficult for Mary.

On one of the center's weekly visits to the park, Mary sat alone on a bench, watching the sun play hide-and-seek behind the clouds. She watched a man walk circles around the track, but did not pay close attention to him as he looked plain.

CHANGING FILTHY GARMENTS

Little did Mary know that who she was watching was not an ordinary man, but rather a prophet of the Most High God. On his fifth lap, the man heard the voice of his Heavenly Father. The tall, slim, gray-haired prophet walked over to Mary, sat down next to her, and inquired about her day.

He introduced himself as Joshua Reuben and she followed his introduction with her own. Mary answered his questions haphazardly, not disclosing too much about herself and her life. While she spoke in a general and cordial way, the Spirit of the Lord spoke to Joshua, and he began to prophesy.

"Mary, I AM says He loves you. The God of Abraham, Isaac, and Jacob has declared His love for you. The Good Shepherd declares His love for you."

Mary said nothing because she didn't want to hear His words through this man. She was perplexed as to how God could love her after she had been so disobedient, rebellious, and angry at Him for so long.

This did not deter the servant of the Most High God from continuing. "I see a Sunday school teacher. She loves God and she loves you. I see her in her prayer room with a tallit on, praying for you early in the morning between 4:00 a.m. and 6:00 a.m. She prays for you both day and night.

"I see a woman who has slept in the Lord. She went to sleep and did not awaken. She adores you and her heart is with you. Her name is written in the Book of Life, and she is now with the Father of lights in paradise. He has wiped away every tear from her eyes; she will no longer see death, mourn, or cry."

Mary realized right away that he was not a false prophet, but rather a true man of God. Deeply moved by his revelation from God, she wept in his arms and let out a loud cry from the depths of her soul.

Joshua consoled her until it was time for her to leave, but the two agreed to meet every Friday at the same bench.

CHAPTER 4

After three months of meeting with Joshua every Friday, Mary began to open up about her disappointments and anger toward God. Over time, her hardened heart softened and became more receptive to God's love. She desired His love over her shame. One Thursday, Joshua asked Benson King, Mary's counselor and immediate supervisor, if she could accompany him to a nearby mountain. Mr. King agreed, and the two drove the hour and a half to the mountain.

When they arrived at the summit of the mountain, the prophet began to speak to her about the knowledge of God. "The Lamb of God received many of His revelations while looking over the Lord's glory from mountain tops. I frequently visit the mountain to commune with my Heavenly Father in order to hear from Him and receive His guidance. I pray in the Spirit, and the Father hears me; He answers my prayers. He frequently reveals information that I am unable to see."

While he was speaking, he heard the Lord and quoted Zechariah 3:3-4 to Mary. "Now Joshua was clothed in filthy garments and stood before the Angel. Then He answered and spoke to those who stood before Him, saying 'Take away his filthy garments from him.' And to him He said, 'See, I have removed your iniquity from you, and I will clothe you with rich robes.'

"As the Lord did for Joshua, he will do for you, Mary," God's servant finished.

Mary fell to her knees and began to cry out to God for mercy. "But I am not worthy!" she sobbed.

CHANGING FILTHY GARMENTS

The man of God assured her that she was. "On the cross, the resurrected One paid the penalty for your sin." As tears continued to stream down her cheeks, Joshua asked her if she would accept Jesus into her heart.

"Yes," she replied, and the man of God led Mary to repentance. On that day, kneeling on the summit of the mountain, Mary surrendered her life to the King of Kings and Lord of Lords. As she repented of her sins and confessed Jesus as Lord of her life, He spoke to her through His messenger.

"'I am the Lord your God; there is no one else! I am faithful and just to forgive your sins and cleanse you from all unrighteousness,' says the Lord!"

The vessel of God rejoiced in Christ as a new member of God's kingdom was added. Mary felt clean on the inside. Weights that had held her down were lifted off, chains were abolished. She was light and free as spotless clouds of brightness smashed the clouds of darkness surrounding her. She looked at her hands as if they were new, not believing how clean she felt. She looked down at her feet, thinking she was floating, but they were firmly planted on the ground. All of the corrosive sins that had bound her were washed away, and a pure spirit rested in her instantly.

Mary couldn't help but wonder as they descended the mountain and asked Joshua, "Do I look different? I don't feel like myself anymore."

Joshua laughed while quoting 2 Corinthians 5:17. "'Therefore, if any of you are in Christ, the new creation has come: the old has passed away, and the new is here!' You have been born again; everything is new. Your body remains the same, but your spirit is alive unto God."

Back at the facility, Mary thanked Mr. King and all of the counselors who encouraged her. She unashamedly announced her new birth in the Messiah with joy. They all rejoiced with her in her new freedom. Mr. King made sure to say, "Don't walk in discouragement. Your past will try to come back to you in these areas."

CHAPTER 4

She was given permission to make a call to Quilla Mae, God's saint. When Quilla Mae heard Mary's voice on the other end of the line, she burst into tears of joy for she hadn't heard from her spiritual daughter in such a long time.

"'If we are faithless, He remains faithful; He cannot disown himself,'" Quilla Mae said, quoting 2 Timothy 2:13. "There were times when I didn't think I'd hear from you again, my dear, but I'd tell myself that God is faithful and keeps His covenant of love for a thousand generations."

Mary repeatedly apologized to Quilla Mae and begged her forgiveness for how she had treated her. Quilla Mae repeatedly told her that she was forgiven, and that God commands His children to forgive, quoting Matthew 6:15. She was just relieved that the woman she loved like a daughter had been found.

Mary gave her a detailed testimony of how God saved her from her many sins. She told her how the prophet Joshua ministered to her. The two discussed what Mary had done over the last ten years. Mary felt ashamed and angry at herself as she talked about what she had done, but the wise elder quickly quoted the Word of God in Lamentations 3:22-23. "'Through the Lord's mercies we are not consumed, because His compassions fail not. They are new every morning; great is Your faithfulness.'"

The two kingdom citizens, one seasoned and the other new, talked for hours about Jesus's mercy and grace. Quilla Mae blessed her at the end of the call and begged Mary to call her daily, weekly, or whenever she could.

When Mary's time at the rehabilitation center ended the following week, the staff was able to secure her a job as a waiter through their connections and transitional housing. She was grateful, and within months of working, God granted Mary favor, allowing her to pay her living expenses and have some money left over.

Mary had never imagined herself as a waitress, but she was grateful to be alive and free of drugs and alcohol. She wanted to work in the communication field because it was her major in school and her passion, but she couldn't until she found work in the industry. So, she stayed at the restaurant. She served her customers with diligence and delight, remembering Colossians 3:23 while she did. *And whatever you do, do it heartily as to the Lord and not to men.*

With that scripture in her heart, her tips were higher than those of her coworkers. She was the best waitress in the restaurant, and the tips she earned allowed her to move into a better one-bedroom apartment.

***

For three years, she praised, worshiped, and thanked God for saving her life, removing her shame, and healing her broken heart. For three years, she was faithful. She was grateful to have been invited to the Lord's wedding feast, and compelled by the Spirit of God, she put on the royal robe of the wedding garment.

The cares of the world no longer concerned her; she no longer lusted after the designer bags, designer clothes, foreign cars, or extravagant parties, and the who's who of the city had been flushed from her system. Her focus was solely on God, and she did not waver during this time of newness. Her feet were firmly planted in the house of God.

She discovered a house of worship close to her apartment. Carefree, she walked and attended service regularly. She thrived in volunteering in every need that the members of the body of Christ asked of her, whether it was cleaning the toilets, ushering people to their seats, being a part of the homeless ministry and the women's ministry, feeding the poor, and clothing the naked.

CHAPTER 4

When the remnant of God called, she was there, and whenever the doors of God's house were opened, she was there.

While serving her customers one day, a woman who could hear the Mighty One of Israel's voice received a message from the Creator. When she finished her meal, she asked for a refill of her soda, and when Mary returned with it, she asked her to take a seat and spoke. "Who is a faithful and wise servant? Well done, good and faithful servant; you were steadfast in a few matters." Mary's face lit up at the prospect of hearing God's Word before the woman continued.

"Precious child of God, the Lord will promote you and grant you your heart's desire. This place can no longer accommodate you. The Spirit of God says in Isaiah 54:2, 'Enlarge the place of your tent, and let them stretch out the curtains of your dwellings; Do not spare; Lengthen your cords, And strengthen your stakes.' He has shown me that you feed the hungry, give drinks to the thirsty, take in strangers, clothe the naked, visit the sick, and look after the imprisoned. You did it all with a pure heart. He'll promote you twenty-one days from now!"

Mary hardly blinked as she was so enthralled by the Word of the Lord. She sowed all of the tips she received that evening, which totaled more than $300.00, into the hands of the woman of God.

Mary returned home that night, ecstatic and eager. She called Quilla Mae to tell her what the woman of God had said. Her spiritual mentor was overjoyed by God's prophecies, and they prayed for His faithfulness. Mary honored God with twice the amount she usually gave in worship service on the advice of her mentor; the offering expressed her gratitude to Him.

God fulfilled His promise in twenty-one days. Mary received a call from one of the companies to which she had applied for an entry-level marketing position. They offered the job on the spot after Mary interviewed over the phone. Mary was overjoyed and praised the living God for giving her the job she had requested of Him.

CHANGING FILTHY GARMENTS

She called Quilla Mae to share the wonderful news. She, in turn, shared Mary's joy and congratulated her while praising God. Quilla Mae prayed for God's favor and blessing on her new job, asking God to bless the works of her hands and grant her success. She made a point of reminding her student of the first fruit offering, telling her to honor God by giving her entire first paycheck for the new job to the house of God or to the priest, and to always honor God by tithing ten percent of all her income. Mary listened to her spiritual mentor and planned to follow through on everything she said.

Mary began her new job at a popular radio station after giving a two-week notice to the restaurant. The only disadvantage of the position was that they played secular music with explicit sexual content, which meant that it would be in her ears all day, but Mary was eager to learn and felt fortunate to be in a field that she desired.

Throughout the days and weeks that followed, Mary's friendly demeanor quickly won the hearts and affection of her coworkers and supervisors. She completed her work with the highest level of quality, above the normal standard, and she exceeded all of their expectations. She walked in a quiet confidence and professionalism, and the God of Abraham, Isaac, and Jacob favored her and everyone at the radio station.

Born again, people could see in Mary crops of love, joy, peace, and faithfulness. When asked about the secret to her success, she boldly and openly confessed, "Yeshua Hamashiach."

She followed Proverbs 3:9. *Honor the Lord with your possessions, and with the first fruits of all your increase; so that your barns will be full of plenty, and your vats will overflow with new wine.*

She was attentive to the Word of the Lord and the teachings of her rabbi and spiritual mentor, adhering to Jehovah Jireh's words in Malachi 3:10 with her biweekly earnings. *"Bring all the tithes into the storehouse, that there may be food in My house,"* says the Lord of hosts, *"and try Me now in*

CHAPTER 4

this, if I will not open for you the windows of heaven and pour out for you such blessing that there will not be room enough to receive it."

With her diligent work ethic and the Lord blessing the works of her hands, she was promoted to manager of marketing and advertising within three years of working at the station. God's favor was evident on her life through obedience and diligence; He had brought her back to a level of life she once chased. The world's influence no longer gripped her with lust and the deception of fullness; instead, she cheerfully gave her resources to things that would please the King. She honored Him through first fruit offerings, tithes, free will offerings, and liberally gave alms to the poor. In return, He added the things she desired.

God rewarded her efforts, and she was able to upgrade from a one-bedroom apartment on the outskirts of town to a lavish condo downtown, and she was able to replace the cars she lost. She prospered, made new friends, and kept the commandments, laws, precepts, and statutes the Lord had written during those three years. Her focus was on her God and her work, and He honored it.

***

In the fourth year, her focus and intensity began to wane. She was lonely and desired the companionship of a mate. A man who she could go to dinner and the movies; a man who loved the Lord and who she could go to the house of worship with. She desired a protector, a provider, a man after God's heart who she could build a life with.

In her solitude, she prayed to God to send the perfect man, the right man, so that her union with seclusion would end. She invited her mentor and the prophet of God to join her in faith, agreeing and believing that her rib would arrive soon.

Both Quilla Mae and Joshua prayed for her, and both heard the voice of God say she would marry because it was His will for her and He would send a man after His own heart to her, but both servants of the Lord warned her to be vigilant and patient, not looking with the eyes of her flesh or in haste, but with the Spirit and patience.

She listened to the voice of Jehovah for a season and prayed daily for her husband, but after months passed, her patience began to wane. She began to ask friends for introductions. She tried speed dating, online Christian dating, but nothing was materializing and she became frustrated. The more she pushed for love, the more she felt alone and despondent.

And then it happened.

A man walked into her office one day at work as she sulked, wondering why God had not answered her prayers. He looked like a million dollars in his suit. Flawless skin, a brilliant smile, and confidence that could fill the entire building.

Mary couldn't take her eyes off of him. He was taller than her ex-husband, standing at six-foot-five or taller. He wore a tailor-made suit with his muscles visible through it; he looked like a stellar athlete. When he smiled, his teeth gleaned with whiteness. His face and hair were like the models seen in magazines. The aroma of his cologne was so strong and pleasant that every woman in the office came to smell it.

Mary was enthralled and lost her senses as she gazed into his eyes. His name was Cain Davis, and he'd come to see Mary specifically about promoting his business on the station. She heard nothing about business, but nodded her head in compliance to everything the man asked, hypnotized by his attractiveness.

Cain was also drawn to Mary. He liked the way her dress hugged her body, each curve perfectly placed. Her toned arms enticed him; her legs were strong and stout. Her stomach was flat, and her backside was curvaceous and beautiful.

CHAPTER 4

"You look so familiar. You sure we've never met before?" Cain asked as he stood up to leave, transfixed by Mary's dazzling skin, stunning hair, and exquisite body.

"Oh, I'd remember you. Believe me," Mary replied, blushing. She didn't mean to be so obvious in her attraction to him, but it was so powerful. She could hardly control herself.

"Fair enough. I hope to speak with you again soon. I would also love to take you out for coffee sometime," he said as he handed her his business card. When he winked at her and turned to walk away, Mary almost passed out.

She called that very night, and she talked to Cain every night after that. They went on their first, second, and third dates. Cain was the gentleman she had prayed for. He constantly complimented her on her beauty and attractiveness. She enjoyed his conversation for he was smart, educated, and well compensated. He was the answer to all of her prayers.

There was only one issue: he had not been saved by grace through Yeshua. It slightly disappointed her when she finally spoke to him about her faith in God, but she believed she could win him to Christ.

She told Quilla Mae about Cain, excited that he was the one she hoped her spiritual mentor would validate and that God would whisper in her ear His approval, but Quilla Mae did not hear the voice of the Lord, so she quietly listened while Mary sung Cain's praises and imagined their future together.

As Mary continued to speak, Quilla Mae asked, "Does he believe in Yeshua?"

Mary initially stammered before responding, "Well... he doesn't believe in God." She promised that the two would start going to worship services together. "I think I can win him over. Isn't that what we're supposed to do as believers? Show the non-believers the way?" She began to worry that her spiritual mentor would reject him if she sensed that they were unequally yoked.

Quilla Mae took a deep breath, and suddenly heard the voice of the Most High in her right ear. "The Lord of Host says, 'This is not your husband. I have not chosen him,'" the women of God said as the Lord had commanded.

Mary's heart sank. She didn't want to hear that he was not the one because he was everything she had wished for: tall, handsome, athletic, smart, funny, financially stable, and extremely capable. She was shattered as Quilla Mae continued to say, "He is not the one. He is not the one."

"But… I can bring him to the Lord," Mary uttered, but Quilla Mae reminded her of her Master's words in 2 Timothy 3:5. *Having a form of godliness but denying its power, and from such people turn away.* When the Lord opened her eyes, she saw that the young man was unwilling to change or repent of his sins.

Mary offered rebuttal, but her elder quickly refuted it, knowing what Mary would say. "Look at our God's Word in 2 Corinthians 6:14. 'Do not be unequally yoked together with unbelievers. For what fellowship does righteousness have with lawlessness, and what communion does light have with darkness?'"

Mary, distraught and irritated, offered no explanation to her mentor. She made excuses to get off the phone and hung up quickly.

Mary was determined to have the man she desired; all she needed was time to lead Cain to Jesus's atoned blood. She continued to date Cain in the hopes that God's word would change, and Cain would give his life to Yeshua the Messiah.

The relationship remained unwavering; she saw him more often, but the God of Israel always confirmed His word, sending His messengers to warn her of the consequences of her disobedience.

One day, Joshua called her. "Mary, the Lord says to you through 1 Corinthians 6:18, 'Flee from fornication and all the sins that so easily besought you. Whoever commits fornication sins against his own body.'"

CHAPTER 4

Mary was already upset by the prophecy from Quilla Mae, but now she was even more upset to hear this new prophecy. "I've been pure since the day I was born again. No man has touched me, and I have not touched a man."

She boldly opposed Joshua's words with confidence for perhaps he and Quilla Mae were not hearing God's voice clearly. Perhaps they were wrong. This only strengthened her resolve to continue her relationship with Cain.

"These are God's words of warning. 'Pride goes before destruction, and a haughty spirit before a fall,'" Joshua said, quoting Proverbs 16:18.

In her flesh, she replied to the prophet, "Sometimes it takes time for people to surrender to God. I ran for years, but I eventually returned to Him. I will encourage Cain and I will lead him. I can't give up on him… I can't give up on us. Cain will return to God, as well."

"He is not the one!" the prophet declared emphatically. "I hear my Father clearly!" This was the first time he ever spoke in this manner. He knew Mary's heart had hardened to the point where she could not refuse Cain. He began to speak in an unknown tongue after he rebuked Mary according to Galatians 5:19. "'Now the works of the flesh are manifest, which are adultery, fornication, uncleanness, and lewdness.'"

Mary didn't say anything else. She was confident in herself and her flesh; she would not break her oath to God to abstain from sex until marriage. She looked to prove both of them wrong by leading Cain to Christ and marrying him. Her angry silence was used as a weapon to show the man of God her displeasure with his reprimand, but instead of ending the call, Joshua continued to quote the Word as the spirit of the Lord gave utterance and he remembered.

"'For this is the will of God, your sanctification, that you abstain from fornication,'" he quoted 1 Thessalonians 4:3-5.

CHANGING FILTHY GARMENTS

Mary did not bother saying goodbye to the prophet; instead, she hung up the phone to express her irritation with his chastisement. She continued to see Cain in her rebellion, enjoying the companionship of the man she had placed her affection on.

CHAPTER 5

Cain and Mary went out to dinner on a Friday night. Afterwards, Cain convinced her to see *The Awakening of Audacity*, a popular movie playing in theaters, and he had bought tickets for the midnight showing.

"I see you're smiling!" Cain said while kissing Mary's cheeks after the movie was over.

"All right, I'll admit it was good." Mary smiled back.

A downpour began as they stepped out from under the theater awning, the rainwater falling like buckets. With no umbrella and their car parked far away, they ran and were drenched from head to toe by the time they reached their car.

Cain suggested they go to his condo to clean up and dry off because it was much closer than hers. He didn't want her to catch a cold or become ill. Mary's head began to ring, her spirit cautioned her not to go, but Cain persisted.

Cain took off his shirt and undershirt as he walked in the door, flexing his extremely muscular chest, forearms, biceps, and rippled abs.

Mary watched carefully as his bulky built chest jumped one peck to the other. She turned her head when Cain caught her starring, but her eyes planted the seed of lust and her flesh became aroused.

Cain insisted she take a shower in the guest bedroom. He went into his closet for towels and clothes for when she was done. Mary set the water to cool, her body hot. She tried to extinguish the flames of her passion as she wanted to be touched, but she couldn't. She imagined Cain touching every part of her anatomy in the shower. It had been so long since she had felt a man's hand on her body.

She turned the shower knob to its highest setting, closed her eyes, and washed herself as if her hands were Cain's. She'd lost self-control and wished Cain would come in as she inappropriately touched herself. Cain was thinking the same thing as the water ran down her black hair, her petite neck, her voluptuous body, her plump breast, her well-rounded buttocks. She was flawless.

Mary looked at him and invited him to join her. They explored each other's bodies in the shower and then continued in the bedroom until the sun rose.

While her body felt stimulated, Mary's spirit mourned. The lust of the flesh had ruled over her even though she had given her life and body to God. Still, she continued to enjoy the sexual acts of illegal privity for the rest of the weekend.

Monday morning, she went to work wearing the same clothes she had worn on Friday. Throughout the day, she was not herself. Her spirit cried in anguish over the sin she had committed against her God. She spent the majority of her day in her office, stricken with grief as she cried over breaking her renewed covenant with God.

When she returned home, she expressed her sorrow to Yeshua. The more she apologized, the heavier her transgression seemed to become. The enemy whispered in her ear that she was unworthy. She began to condemn herself, angry that she had grieved the Holy Spirit. She became increasingly unforgiving, and it enraged her that she had allowed herself to become entangled in the bondage of sin again. When the phone rang, she told herself that she would end her relationship with Cain immediately.

CHAPTER 5

"What's the matter? Are you okay?" Cain inquired.

"No," Mary cried. She assured him that what had occurred could never happen again. "I am a child of God. I have been born again, and I have grieved the Spirit of God."

Cain apologized and asked if he could come over. Mary did not agree and told him no, but after several attempts, Mary relented from her firm stance. Cain arrived with a bouquet of roses which Mary accepted. The scent of his cologne overpowered the scent of the roses and flooded her nostrils as he kissed her on the check once she let him in the door.

Cain apologized once more for what had happened, telling her that she didn't have to be ashamed because it was natural between two people who were attracted to each other and who were falling in love. He suggested that God wasn't mad at them, but Mary knew he was wrong. God's will was for men and women to be married before having sex, but her itchy ears couldn't ignore Cain's mention of the word love.

"Do you love me?" she asked, knowing she was in love with him. Cain grabbed her hands and said, "I'm falling in love with you, Mary."

"I love you, too, Cain," she tearfully replied.

He kissed her passionately and quickly scooped her up off her feet, whisking her away to her room where the two had sex once more. Immediately after Cain left, Mary's heart was filled with sorrow again. She despised what she was doing. She knew it displeased God. Her spirit bore witness to it, but she couldn't bring her lust under control. Her spirit was willing, but her flesh was weak.

The more she fought against her flesh, the more the flesh won, causing her to withdraw from God. Her attendance in His house—once faithful on Wednesdays, Saturdays, and Sundays—was now neglected due to her entwinement with Cain.

She gave up her duties of ushering and cleaning God's house. She refused to be a part of the prayer team. She abandoned the sick and shut in. Feeding the hungry and clothing the naked interfered with her time with Cain, so she ended it. The longer she stayed with Cain, the more she engaged in forbidden sex until she no longer felt guilty of her sin, reasoning with herself that Cain would marry her, and the sin would be reconciled.

When Quilla Mae, Joshua, and others from her congregation called, she did not answer, and when they left messages, they were not returned. For months, Mary lived in a backslidden state, indulging in every fleshly desire. She and Cain began to lay together every night, regardless of who's house it was.

Cain suggested watching pornography with Mary during one of their sex sessions to spice things up. Mary didn't want to return to the chains from which God had delivered her, but she did so to please Cain. While they watched, memories of the life she left behind began to flood in. She remembered her ex and all of her male and female partners she worked with during her time in the industry.

When a scene of her appeared on the screen, she felt small and embarrassed. She cried of humiliation as she did not want her future husband to see her with multiple partners or witness her at her lowest point in life.

"That's why you looked so familiar!" Cain exclaimed as he stood up. "You used to work in porn! I bet you've been with a lot of people, huh? When were you going to tell me?" "After I married you?"

He was furious and rushed to put on his clothes.

"Please, Cain. This is all in the past. I no longer do that. I have changed; I am saved. I'm not that woman anymore!" Mary said as she sobbed for him.

CHAPTER 5

Cain took his keys. "I'm going for a walk. Please don't be here when I return," he said as he slammed the door shut behind him. Trembling, Mary placed her clothes on and made her way out of his home.

She was broken. She believed Cain was the answer to her prayers despite the Lord's word from Quilla Mae and Joshua, but she couldn't give up. She loved him and if he had an ounce of compassion and forgiveness in him, they could be truly free of her past sins.

Cain called Mary that night. He apologized for what he said and the manner in which he stormed out. In Cain's heart, he told himself that he could never marry her and that she could never bear his children. Seeing her with other men and women made him feel ashamed to be with her.

To save the relationship, Mary suggested they go to counseling. Cain did not want to stop seeing her for he was having the best sex he had ever had in his life, but he began to distance himself emotionally and affectionately. He stopped taking her to the movies, sporting events, shows, and dinners. There were no more peaceful walks in the park, and the only time he called was for sex.

Having had sex professionally, she could tell when it was just business by the way he touched her. There was no love, just causal sex. She, however, loved him and fought hard for counseling as well as his attendance to God's house.

He eventually agreed to counseling and they met every Thursday for an hour and a half. The first two sessions went exceptionally well. Cain said all of the right things as he confessed his feelings for her. Because weekly worship services were important to Mary, the counselor suggested they attend them.

Pastor Peter and the majority of the congregation welcomed Mary back with open arms, telling her how much they loved and missed her, but there were some who did not feel the same way, they strongly opposed her being allowed back into fold believing that she should be condemned for her absence. Overall, she received love and belonging in a friendly manner. She was happy to be planted back in the house of God alongside Cain, her hopeful future husband, and believed that her life was on the way to returning to normal.

Cain's personality quickly won him friends within the men's ministry, and they welcomed him with open arms. In this coterie environment, he was able to open up and discuss all of the issues and antipathy that plagued his and Mary's relationship. After several weeks of open dialogue, he revealed to the men his dilemma of Mary being a former porn star.

The men were taken back. Some immediately informed their wives of the news, and like wildfire, gossip quickly spread throughout the church. Many people investigated and discovered that it was true, and some openly inquired to Mary, making her feel ashamed of her previous deeds.

Mary's body went numb, her heart sunk into her stomach, and she ran out of the sanctuary, unable to believe Cain would tell her story.

She wanted to crawl under a rock and die when she got home, the shame and guilt were so overwhelming. She cried in her bed as Cain called and called, but she refused to answer. When he arrived at her house, she did not respond. She was so angry at him that she did not want to see him again.

At the advice of the counselor, Mary met with Cain for their next counseling session, but she lashed out at him for being naive enough to tell her privacy in a public setting.

Cain flew off the handle, unable to bear the sting of her past. "I can't do this!" he exclaimed. "What will my parents say if I marry a former porn star? What are we going to tell our children? I can't go through life with everyone having seen my wife with multiple men and women. It's humiliating! I can't do! It is over!"

CHAPTER 5

He abruptly walked out. Mary shook in anger The counselor tried to console her, but she refused. Empty tears rolled down her cheeks as she remembered the prophecies foretold by Quilla Mae and Joshua. Humiliated, she walked out.

When she arrived home, she laid on her bed, too proud to call on the name of the Lord or the people He called His servants. Depressed, she took vacation days off from work, the only places she went being the bathroom and her bedroom.

She returned to work after a few days, brokenhearted and depressed. Her coworkers could see her dismay every morning as the once jovial and quick-witted woman now walked joyless.

Brian Douglas, her subordinate, could see his supervisor was not right. Like her, he was a believer in Jesus, so he decided to give her biblical advice. He walked into her office with his pocket bible snuggly tucked his suit coat he began.

"When I first met you, you only talked about God. I was so moved by your faith and how openly you expressed your love for Jesus. Return to God and return to His love, break free from this shackle."

He took his Bible out, flipped to a seemingly random page, and began reading. "'Yet I will rejoice in the Lord, I will rejoice in the God of my salvation,' says Habakkuk 3:18." He paused and flipped to another part of his Bible. "'Get back to your strength the joy of the Lord. Do as our King says in Hosea 14:1, 'Return to the Lord your God, for you have stumbled because of your iniquity.' If you do, God will make Joel 2:13 manifest in your life."

Without missing a beat, Brian flipped to the Book of Joel as the Holy Spirit guided him. "'So rend your heart, not your garments; return to the Lord your God, for He is gracious and merciful, slow to anger and great in kindness, and He refrains from harming.'"

CHANGING FILTHY GARMENTS

Brian had always been mute during meetings and conference calls, and he barely spoke during his evaluations. It was only fitting Mary's jaw dropped as she could only stare in awe as he continued speaking God's Word to her. She had no idea he was a follower of Jesus.

She returned home, she clothed herself in the spirit of sackcloth, and laid prostrate before the Lord. Lamenting herself in repentance, she cried out to God for His compassion and forgiveness. She confessed her sins and iniquities, and wept bitterly before the altar, confessing all of her transgressions.

When she stood up, she vowed in her heart that she would never commit fornication again, and the next intercourse she would have would be in an undefiled bed with her husband.

With her mind transformed and her spirited renewed, she prayed the prayer of King David. "'Create in me a clean heart, O God, and renew a steadfast spirit within me,'" she quoted Psalm 51:10 over and over again.

The merciful Master restored the joy of her salvation, and she rededicated her life to Him. She returned to His presence, and He accepted her as His daughter.

****

Sunday morning, Mary arrived early at her King's house, eager to be in His presence. She sat in the first pew, glad to be back. She sung with vigor and passion as the praise team led worship, raising her voice to the King of Kings and Lord of Lords. As she sung from the depths of her soul, she could feel the penetrating daggers of judgment. Some members of the congregation looked down on her with disgust, despising her for returning to the house of prayer and worshiping God. They conducted themselves as Pharisees and scribes loving judgment over mercy.

CHAPTER 5

When the psalmists finished their worship to the Holy One of Israel, Pastor Peter approached the podium slowly to deliver the message the Most High had given him. He affixed the microphone to his liking and announced the message's preamble.

"The message our God has given today is 'backslidden.'" The Pharisees and scribes erupted in applause and cheered. They hoped the pastor would expel Mary from the congregation. They screamed hallelujah with contempt and said among themselves, with self-righteousness, that she was despicable.

Mary's shoulders sagged as she couldn't help feeling two feet tall. Her face turned bright red as she listened to the scornful laughter of those she had considered her spiritual family like the Beverly sisters, the Washingtons, and the Cohens'. They intensified their starring and their gazes seemed to pierce right through her. She wanted to get up and leave, but being in the first row, she was forced to stay. Nervous, her hands began to sweat.

"Let us consider a couple of backslidden scriptures. In Proverbs 26:11, it says, 'As a dog returns to his own vomit, so a fool repeats his folly.'"

The Pharisees clapped with enthusiasm while the spirit in Mary dropped.

"Hosea 11:7," the pastor continued. "'My people are bent on backsliding from Me. Though they call to the Most High, None at all exalt Him.'"

The unforgiven nodded in agreement. More scripture was read by the pastor.

"Turn to Jeremiah 5:6 and 7 in your Bibles. 'Therefore, a lion from the forest shall slay them; a leopard will watch over their cities. Everyone who goes out from there shall be torn in pieces, because their transgression are many; Their backslidings have increased. How shall I pardon you for this? Your children have forsaken Me and sworn by those that are not gods. When I had fed them to the full, then they committed adultery and assembled themselves by troops in the harlot's houses.'"

CHANGING FILTHY GARMENTS

The man of God paused. The merciless were in a frenzy, standing in agreement and clapping feverishly. Mary kept her gaze fixed on the pastor, but her eyes filled with tears as shame and guilt swelled within her heart, knowing that the next words of the pastor would almost certainly result in her expulsion.

Pastor Peter met Mary's gaze directly. "The title of today's message is 'Grace for the Backslider.'"

The loveless were perplexed when they heard this and sat down, perturbed. The messenger of God continued. "Our God is a loving God full of compassion and merciful in all His ways. It says in Lamentations 3:22, 'Through the Lord's mercies we are not consumed because his compassions fail not.'"

Mary's head began to lift.

"'The Lord is merciful and gracious, slow to anger and abounding in mercy,' Psalm 103:8 declares."

Mary sat on the edge of her seat, tears streaming down her face as she whispered to herself, "*Baruch atah Adonai, Eloheinu Melech ha'olam*," thanking Him for His unfailing love.

The injudicious gawked at the man of God, but the preacher did not back down despite their displeasure. "'But He, being full of compassion, forgave their iniquity, and did not destroy them,'" says the God of wonders in Psalm 78:38. Yes, many times He turned His anger away, and did not stir up His wrath.

"I speak to all who have led a sinful lifestyle and those who have backslidden that the God of Israel, the God of Abraham, Isaac, and Jacob loves you. The Rose of Sharon, Yeshua is His name, He wants you back! Return to His loving embrace. He will welcome you with open arms as He did the Prodigal Son in Luke 15:20."

The man of God stirred up the Spirit that dwelled in him and began to speak in tongues of fire. Mary rose to her feet, lifted up her arms in worship to the heavens, and received the Father's love.

CHAPTER 5

The true body of Christ wept, worshipped, and sang praises to the King as the Spirit of God filled the tabernacle. The Beverly sisters, the Washingtons, and the Cohens looked on disgruntled, but the flow of the spirit continued in His house.

"The ox kept treading out the grain. People of God, the Lord says to you in Jeremiah 3:14, " Return, O backsliding children, says the Lord; " for I am married to you. I will take you, one from a city and two from a family, and I will bring you to Zion"

As the Spirit spoke, Pastor Peter continued to speak boldly. "The Lord says to you, beloved, in Hosea 2:19, "I will betroth you to Me forever; Yes, I will betroth you to Me In righteousness and justice, In lovingkindness and mercy;" he gave a moment for selah before proclaiming "For all have sinned and fall short of God's glory."

Those who received the Messiah's atonement and were forgiven wept in His presence. The congregation sang a new song to their Lord, and from the front pews to the back, believers danced, shouted, and lay prostrate in awe of His compassion as His Glory filled His house.

The pastor attempted to continue preaching, but the weight of the King's glory was too much for him. He fell to both knees, unable to speak, and could only raise his hands in honor to the One who had called him.

The congregation worshiped for hours on end. No one complained or considered leaving as the true believers in Him enjoyed the majestic glory of their King.

When the cloud of glory began to dissipate, Pastor Peter stood up and invited everyone to accept Jesus Christ as their personal Savior. Those who had fallen away were invited to return to their Heavenly Father's love.

"If you have backslidden like me before, come to the front!" he exclaimed enthusiastically. Mary wasted no time and was the first person at the altar. Pastor Peter smiled at her and quoted part of Jeremiah 3:14 again. "'Turn, O backsliding children, for I am married to you,' says the Lord."

Happy, he shouted to the congregation with a loud voice, "He loves you, backslider! He is married to you! Come back to Him and He will receive you with tender love and kindness! He has not given up on you and He loves you! Receive His compassion!"

With his earnest plea, people who were in a backslidden state and those who had not received Yeshua Messiah were given the opportunity to do so. People accepted Jesus's blood as an atonement for their sins while those who were tired of being lukewarm wanted to be on fire for God.

So, they repented and gave their lives to the Good Shepherd, many on their knees. The kingdom of God received new citizens and prodigal sons and daughters, the earthly shepherd shed tears of joy, and all of heaven rejoiced as many names were added to the Book of Life.

With God's grace pouring down on His people, Pastor Peter came down and prayed individually for each person, leading them in repentance.

"John 3:16, 'For God so loved the world that He gave His only begotten Son, that whoever believes in Him should not perish but have everlasting life.'"

He anointed the new converts in Christ with oil in his left hand and with his right index finger placed the mark of Christ on their foreheads. Moving through the crowd, the man of God began to tire, but the Lord told him to keep speaking, so with more compassionate, he spoke the Word of the Lord.

"Isaiah 1:18, 'Come now, and let us reason together', Says the Lord, " Though your sins are like scarlet, They shall be as white as snow; Though they are red like crimson, They shall be as wool." Isaiah 43:25, 'I, even I, am He who blots out your transgressions for my own sake; And I will not remember your sins." Just as Adonai said to the woman in Luke 7:48, 'Then He said to her, Your sins are forgiven!'"

CHAPTER 5

Those who needed mercy and grace received it, then they walked joyfully to their seats, free of all of their trespasses and chains. Mary hugged the man of God, but he did not allow her to return right away, asking her, instead, to wait.

He cited Psalm 107:2. "'Let the Lord's redeemed say so, whom He has redeemed from the hand of the enemy.' When those who judge you gossip about you, slander you, or make false accusations about your past, quote this scripture to them. Let the Lord's redeemed say so, then say 'so' as loudly as you can to let them know you've been redeemed by the blood of the Lamb. As the Lord says in Romans 8:1, 'For there is now no condemnation to those who are in Christ Jesus, who do not walk according to the flesh, but according to the Spirit.'"

When he had finally finished, Pastor Peter looked with sternness and disdain at the unloving, uncompassionate, and judgmental so-called people of God. Mary laughed happily as she received the Lord's Word. She returned to her seat with dignity and honor, knowing that God had redeemed her.

When Mary returned home, she immediately called Quilla Mae, who hollered with joy to hear the voice of her daughter. Mary apologized to her spiritual mentor, saying she was sorry. She had repented before God and now wanted to repent to her. Quilla Mae forgave her as she was so relieved and thrilled that Mary was back home in the arms of a loving God.

"Mary, I adore you! I have always loved you and will always love you. As the Bible says in Matthew 18:22, 'seventy times seven is how much I will forgive you and love you.'"

Mary finally accepted Quilla Mae's forgiveness, and she tried to articulate the Lord's grace, mercy, compassion, and forgiveness.

Next, she called God's prophet to repent. Joshua responded with similar joy, quoting Psalm 63:3, "'Father, Your lovingkindness is better than life; my lips will praise You.'" As she had done with Quilla Mae, Mary asked for forgiveness, but the servant of God refused.

"My Heavenly Father will not forgive my sins if I do not forgive the sins of others. I have prayed for you, and I know the Lord will return you to His bosom."

Mary poured out her soul to the prophet, just as she had done to her spiritual mentor. As the prophet listened intently, he spoke words of encouragement and edification to her. He heard the voice of his Father and kept it to himself, but the Lord strongly compelled him to speak the word of knowledge.

"Continue in the house of the Lord where you worship," he said, adding nothing and taking nothing away from what the Lord commanded. "There are serpents biting at you with malice, looking at you spitefully, hurling vicious words at you with their venom, looking to destroy you."

Since her past had been revealed, many wolves in sheep's clothing had come calling her derogatory names such as slut, tramp, and whore. When he heard what the self-proclaimed children of God were saying, the man of God wept.

"These people are not of God. His people walk in love and mercy. They are quick to forgive and they are encouragers and edifiers. Do not listen to them. You are a born-again child of God, and your past has been washed in the blood of the Lamb!

"Don't resent them, don't despise them, for the spirit of the Lord says in Psalm 23:5, 'I will prepare a table before you in the presence of your enemies, anoint your head with oil, and your cup will run over with goodness and mercy for the rest of your days.' The Father says He is looking for those who will worship Him in spirit and truth. Many have gotten bogged down with man-made dogmas. They hurt His people with religious practices not authorized by Him and they teach precepts that are not in His Word nor sanctioned by Him. 'These people draw near to me with their mouths, and honor Me with their lips, but their hearts are far from Me,' says Adonai in Matthew 15:8."

CHAPTER 5

Hearing clearly and full of the Spirit, Joshua prophesied, "Your Boaz will soon find you, and Jehovah Jireh will quickly remove you from your job." When the prophet finished speaking everything that God had told him, he hung up the phone. Mary was happy to receive the word, but she didn't want to yearn and be anxious like she had before.

She was more concerned with rededicating, renewing, and refocusing her relationship with Christ. She walked as a child of light once more, returning to the things that gave her joy and made Him smile.

Back in Elohim's glory, she studied the Word of God more, prayed more, and increased her acts of righteousness. She began to seek out faithful charitable organizations, gave first fruit three times a year, and continued to honor Him with tithes and offerings despite being constantly heckled with vile and contentious slurs. The Father of lights gave her peace in this season, and she could now add another name to God. Jehovah Shalom, the Lord is peace, for He gave her peace for the rest of the year.

***

After a year of restoration and peace, Quilla Mae flew to California. Mary needed to be baptized, fully immersed in the waters the Lord had created. Together with the prophet Joshua, they drove the coast to the ocean's waters, but before they arrived, the prophet of God had to share the word he received for Mary.

"Soon you will leave your job, and He will give you the grace to be a light to women all over the world. A light to those who have been abused, shamed, those who cry for help, and are brokenhearted. The Lord of Hosts will bring them to you in His love, and you will comfort, restore, and build them up. No government system or agency can do what the Lord can do. He is calling you to raise women in His image, women of righteousness and holiness, women of truth, women who will reflect His glory."

Mary wondered how this would be accomplished and when it would be done. Where would she begin? How much would it cost? She didn't have the funds to partake in such a large vision.

As if God was thinking her thoughts, God's prophet responded to her concerns, saying, "In due season, the ancient of days will bring this to pass. Don't worry about who, when, what, where, or how for thus saith the Lord in Numbers 23:19, 'I will perform that good thing which I have promised for I am not a man, that I should lie nor a son of man that I should repent.'"

Mary believed the words of the man of God. She had learned her lesson for not believing.

Still driving, the Lord opened Joshua's eyes. "I see your husband coming in the Spirit. He is a simple man before the Lord, upright and fearful," Joshua said. "You two are getting married soon, and I see a boy and a girl in your arms."

Mary's heart skipped a beat. She was tired of being alone and had desired a husband for so long. As she pondered him in her thoughts, Joshua continued.

"He will meet you with water. Do not mock him because this is the man who God has chosen for you."

Mary wondered why she would mock him. She was still praying for her heart's desire: an over six-foot muscular, athletic, handsome, smart, and rich man who loved the Lord.

The prophet never clarified the water, and she didn't ask for she counted him a true prophet and believed in his words.

Elders from Mary's church awaited their arrival on the beach. When Mary entered the blessedly calm ocean with Quill Mae and Joshua, the elders sang songs of praise to God, asking Him to manifest His presence.

CHAPTER 5

Mary asked her spiritual mentor to baptize her while standing waist-high in the water. Quilla Mae placed her left hand on the lower part of Mary's back, her right hand over her forehead, and Joshua placed his right hand on Quilla Mae's right shoulder while the woman of God prayed.

"Mary Jacobs, I baptize you in the name of the Father, Son, and Holy Ghost in the name of Yeshua Hamashiach, our Lord and Savior in accordance with Galatians 3:27, which says, 'for all of the who were baptized into Christ have clothed yourselves with Christ.'"

She lowered her spiritual daughter under the water for a few seconds and then raised her up. Joshua agreed with her prayer and when he said amen, he began to speak in the mystery of the Spirit, which gave him utterance.

Quilla Mae, stirred by the Spirit of God, submerged Mary once more beneath the waters God created.

"According to John 3:5, 'Jesus answered most assuredly, I say to you unless one is born of water and the spirit, he cannot enter the kingdom of God.' May you enter His kingdom, my daughter," Quilla Mae prayed.

Quilla Mae quoted 1 Peter 3:21. "'There is also an antitype which now saves us- baptism (not the removal of filth of the flesh, but the answer of a good conscience toward God), through the resurrection of Jesus Christ.'"

"Halleluiah!" Mary exclaimed as she emerged from the water. "All praise belongs to God, the God of Abraham, Isaac, and Jacob, the living water, the God of Israel!"

The elders joined her in praise, raising their voices to the Most High and all began to offer her different prophesies granted to them by God.

"Your husband is a God-fearing man who loves the Lord. He has a similar background to you, but God has healed him. The Most High is directing his steps toward you, and he will appear soon."

"Don't let your anger consume you. I see people in the congregation verbally assaulting you, insulting and shaming you on a regular basis. Don't lash out at them; instead, pray for them and speak blessings on them."

"The enemy wants to use your anger as a legal loophole to enter back into your life. Don't allow him access".

"Satan seeks to reclaim you for his kingdom of darkness through anger, but we bind every wile of the enemy in the mighty name of Jesus the Christ."

"Your husband will join you in doing ministry. He has prayed for you for years. He will know your past, but his love, mercy, and compassion for you will be like Christ."

"He will not be what you have prayed for. What you desire is that of the flesh. The one that Adonai has ordained is a ruddy man. He is not six feet tall. He does not have muscles. He is ruddy, but handsome. He loves God and will treat you like a queen. His love for you will be like the love God has for the church as it reads in Ephesians 5:25. 'Husbands, love your wives, just as Christ also loved the church and gave Himself for her.'"

The prophet of God came to a halt so that he could clearly hear his Father. Quilla Mae could hear everything the Most High said to His servants and confirmed every word with a nod of her head.

Joshua continued to prophesy with his eyes open and his mind clear. He could see the outreach program. He could see domestic and international facilities. Mary was a beacon of light to millions of women who were wounded, confused, angry, depressed, and misguided. These women ran to the rivers of flowing water so they would never thirst again.

"This has come again," Joshua said. "I see women from all over the world coming to you. I see multiple buildings all over the world. These women receive Yeshua and are saved by grace. They are on fire for God as I see them praising God and thanking you for your obedience to Christ.

"Very soon, He will grant you the vision, desire, and passion to bring this to fruition. You will wonder where the initial funds came from. It will be introduced to you by a wealthy believer. His daughter's story is your story, and he will be your initial funding after the saints will sow lavishly into this ground, for this is good ground! They will sow abundantly on a daily, weekly, and monthly basis! You will never have to think about finances because Jehovah Jireh will provide for you and the program!"

Mary, Quilla Mae, and the elders were all astounded by the words of knowledge. With final words of grace, they parted and returned to their peaceful lives.

Mary expected God to move quickly when it came to bringing her husband into her life, but God had not deemed it time yet. Months passed, but instead of attempting to make things happen as she had previously done, she read 1 Samuel 12:16. *Now, stand and witness this great thing that the Lord will do before your eyes.*

She read this scripture every day, hoping that any day would be the day, and when the day came and went with no husband, she read Numbers 23:19. This would give her peace and confidence in God. Then she remembered what He said in 2 Peter 3:8. *But, beloved, do not forget this one thing, that with the Lord one day is as a thousand years, and a thousand yours as one day.*

She jokingly asked Adonai if that each day could be the day because she didn't think she could wait a thousand years, but she counted it as joy knowing the Lord was not slack about His promises to her.

She concentrated on her work and her ministry, volunteering at the women's homeless shelter every other day and every Saturday. She treasured her relationships with the women; their stories were her story. She had no father, a drug-addicted mother, and a grandmother who acted as a mother.

Many others, like her, had been abused and raped by their mother's boyfriend or family members. She could relate to their emotional and physical depression, their drug addiction, their hypersexual behavior, and their rage, fury, anger, and madness.

Mary was, unfortunately, frequently muzzled from sharing the message of the Redeemer as the shelter would not allow talks of God; however, it did not stop her from quietly and secretly ministering to the women when she could.

Jesus Christ was their shelter, the only Deliverer who could break the chains off their minds, the only One who could free them from the emotional tricks of the oppressor, Satan. The One who could lift them out of the terrible pit, through the miry clay, and set their feet on solid rock. She wanted to shout out loud that Yeshua was His name, that He had saved her, and that He wanted to save them, too, but the shelter warned her not to spread the message of God's salvation.

Mary realized that in order for the women's lives to be truly transformed, for them to be truly healed from their pasts, and for them to be truly free of drugs and alcohol, the gospel of Christ had to be preached. The One who was excellent, the One who was all knowing, the One who was compassionate, merciful, and loving. The everlasting God; He could take their pain away. They needed the One who created them to speak to their spirits, souls, and hearts.

The more she talked to them and heard their stories, the clearer the vision became, and the more the passion burned. She was tired of ministering in secret; she wanted to minister loudly so the world could hear the God who could raise heads.

After she finished volunteering at the shelter on a Friday night, Mary was walking to her car when she heard a muffled scream. She walked closer to investigate an altercation between a man and a woman. After seeing what was going on, it was obvious the man was planning to rape the defenseless woman. He ripped her shirt and bra off, exposing her breasts, and pulled her pants and panties down with his strong hands.

Mary erupted in rage, recalling all of her emotions from being raped multiple times, and dashed to the aid of the young women. She pounced on the attacker with ferocity, each punch expressing her rage. She struck the rapist in the back, the head, the shoulders, and anywhere else she could reach.

Her punches irritated the large, husky man, and he turned around and slapped her to the ground. "Your next!" he yelled at her. His voice sounded like the voice of many demons and frightened her for a moment, but Mary mustered the courage to stand and fight back as the perpetrator returned his attention to the young woman, ready to penetrate her like a diseased demented dog.

Mary grabbed him by the ankles. Irritated by Mary's refusal to quit, the man turned, drew his arm back, and balled his fist. Mary closed her eyes in anticipation of the blow, but the blow never came as the sounds of running footsteps and the grunts of a struggle stopped the attack. Mary's eyes shot open, revealing a new man who had seemed to appear out of nowhere and had tackled the rapist to the ground.

The assailant was able to free himself from the hero's arms and flee. The brave man called the police and stayed with Mary and the other woman until the authorities arrived.

They were cleared from the medical team after the authorities took their statements. Law enforcement officers escorted the young shaken and terrified woman home.

Mary remained at the scene, enraged by the incident. "I hope they catch him!" she exclaimed. "You know guys like that should be..." she paused, aware that her rage had overcome her, but the man understood what she meant.

"They have no idea about the anxiety, panic attacks, depression, self-blame, anger, and rage that comes with being raped!" Mary couldn't help but scream at the top of her lungs. The incident had triggered her post-traumatic stress disorder. She wiped her tears away as she relived the horrific taking of her innocence.

In order to calm Mary down, the hero asked if he could pray for her. He grabbed Mary's hands, and they closed their eyes. She took a deep breath and fixed her gaze on Jehovah Shalom while the man said a prayer.

"Your Word says You will keep him in perfect peace who keeps his mind fixed on You. Father, we ask for peace now. Jesus, let mercy and truth meet, let righteousness and peace kiss.

"I rebuke the plan of darkness. I call on peace to dwell in this woman. Anxiety, you must flee. Fear, you must bow. Anger, you must be destroyed. The peace that surpasses all comprehension reign in her now."

Mary's tears seized, her rage calmed, and a great peace overshadowed her. The ruddy brown-eyed handsome man of God could see the Good Shepherd's peace resonating in His workmanship, and she smiled while still holding his hands tightly.

They talked and it was therapeutic for Mary to tell her story. The man's name was Luke Phillips and he told her how he was molested as a child and how God delivered him from the emotional and psychological trauma.

"I curse the seed of bitterness to the root in the name of Jesus. Wrath and anger has no place in the life of a child of God, no place in the temple that the Lord has made," he prayed.

He wasn't six feet tall or athletic with muscles. He did not have a six pack. In fact, his stomach bulged out a little, but he had a heart for God. He loved God, and it was evident in his prayers he wasn't lukewarm, but on fire for God.

Mary liked that about him, so she agreed to join him for coffee at the nearby coffee shop. The two spoke as if they had known each other their entire lives; their conversation flowed instantly, and they became best friends.

CHAPTER 5

They revealed all of their ups and downs, their successes and failures. They openly discussed their dark moments of rape and molestation without shame. They discussed the trauma and the cure: Jesus Christ, the hope of Glory!

They talked for hours about the wonderful light that was Yeshua and how without His grace, they couldn't get out of their depression, fear, and anxiety. The conversation lasted until closing time, when the staff had to kick them out because they refused to leave.

Luke was unlike any other man she had ever met. He was humble and meek, a great listener, and his conversations were full of grace. His tongue was a tree of life, and he spoke with God's wisdom. Not to mention he was a doctor and used his medical and spiritual skills to help patients in their recovery.

Luke was smitten by the way Mary's eyes lit up when she spoke about God's mercy and grace, and he couldn't deny that she was even more beautiful in person than she was on film. Earlier in his life, he had turned to porn as a release from what he had gone through and had seen many if not all of her films. Now, he wanted to know more about her, the real her, so he asked for her phone number, which she gladly provided.

CHAPTER 6

Over the next few weeks, Mary and Luke communicated on a daily basis. When they weren't on the phone for hours, they were at the movies or out to dinner. When they weren't out having fun, they served at the shelter, providing food, clothes, hygiene items, and alms.

As their friendship grew, they were able to speak openly and honestly about their trauma, which was beneficial to them both. It was good to talk to someone who would not judge or blame, but who would fully comprehend what each had to overcome like the emotions of rage, anxiety, and fear, as well as an addiction to pornography.

The time they spent together was peaceful and joyous. They never discussed sex and no sexual fantasies entered their minds; they simply enjoyed being friends while serving the lost and worshiping and praying together.

One Friday night, Mary stopped by the shelter to bring food and clothes. As she was pulling in, it was like déjà vu as she saw another young woman in the alley wailing and slumped on the ground, her clothes torn. Mary knew that cry for she had cried that cry countless times before. A woman had been raped, most likely by the last scoundrel whose last attempt she had foiled, but this time, the assailant had succeeded in taking the young woman's innocence with him.

Mary could only embrace the young women while she cried uncontrollably. The rage she felt when she was raped swelled up in her. She wanted the man to feel the violation that she had felt and the violation the precious woman cradled in her arms currently felt.

She took the woman to the police station, but there wasn't much they could do. She didn't have an accurate description and it would take days before DNA samples would come back from their vast database of criminals. They left the station even more perplexed by the ordeal.

On the way home, she felt a burden that she needed to do something. The time for her ministry to be born had come, but she still didn't have the funds to open a facility; the real estate alone would cost a millions of dollars.

She entertained getting a loan, but lacked both assets and liquidity. She refused to accept government assistance because she wanted to be free to preach what the Lord said. She knew very well no government curriculum, human intelligence, or man-made wisdom could redeem lost souls, hurt hearts, and broken spirits.

Frustrated, she prayed to God for guidance. "What should I do? Where do I begin?" she asked aloud in her car. The burden was too great for her to turn her back on, and the flame ignited her desire to protect, cure, and free women.

From Friday night to Sunday morning, her anger went unquenched. She took that rage to morning worship. Her mockers were waiting for her, as always, ready to hurl insults and shameful remarks. They expected Mary to respond with Psalm 107:2, as Pastor Peter had told her to that fateful day, but she did not. Instead, she lashed out at them in anger, cursing them in God's house.

Emboldened by her rage, caustic profanity poured out of her mouth as she screamed at the top of her lungs. She had to be picked up and escorted out of the sanctuary by ushers.

Outside, she could still be heard yelling at the scribes and Pharisees. After she regained her composure, the remnants who loved God were finally able to calm her down.

CHAPTER 6

They put her in her car, and she cried the entire drive home. When Quilla Mae called, she didn't answer. When Joshua called, she didn't answer. When Luke called, she didn't answer. She lay in bed, wondering if she would ever attend that assembly again.

On Wednesday night, after she reconnected with herself, she returned Joshua's call, to which he responded, "Didn't I warn you not to let the enemy in through anger? You have let him in and you have omitted sin in your flesh. I pray that the Lord will raise a standard for you."

The prophet abruptly hung up the phone, but Mary was not offended as she had reasoned to herself that she had done the right thing. Those who judged her deserved it. She had endured their attacks and scorn for far too long, and she felt no remorse for what she had said.

She prayed to God, turned on her TV, and went to sleep. While she slept peacefully, demons entered her dream with sexual fantasies, showing her sex partners she had once been with, both male and female. She was asleep, but conscious of what was happening. Her spirit warred against the sexual immorality, but her flesh was weakening.

The demons spoke dirty words and showed her fantasies, even Cain. He seemed so real in his touch; so real he whispered in her ear. The more her flesh yielded, the more the demons enchanted her with fantasies.

She immediately woke up and took a shower to cleanse herself of the lust she had allowed the enemy to tempt her with. She apologized to God for being complicit in the dream while fully aware of what was going on and not fighting the enemy to wake up.

She went about her life for the next week, going to work, working at the shelter, and talking to Luke. She was relieved when Pastor Peter called to tell her that those who mocked her had been expelled from the congregation, but she still had sexual dreams, and despite her prayers, they came every night.

Seduced by demons in her dreams with sexual sin on a nightly basis, she began to touch herself, knowing she was committing the sin of masturbation. She begged the Father to remove her sexual immorality, feeling ashamed, angry, and unworthy of His grace and mercy.

During breakfast, her phone rang; it was Quilla Mae. Mary let the phone go to voicemail as she was irritated from not sleeping all night and did not want to be chastised.

She told herself she'd call her back at lunch, but the woman of God didn't leave a voicemail, so Mary assumed it was a strong chastisement from God.

Quilla Mae called again after Mary had finished her breakfast. She was still unsure whether she should answer, but after the fifth ring, she decided to. Expecting to be chastised and lectured, she was surprised when she was met with God's love and grace.

"Blessed be the name of the Lord now and forevermore," Quilla Mae praised. "The Lord gives favor and honor. Mary, God is showing His favor to you this morning. He spoke to me and said you will be married soon! He is a great man, a gentle man, a man after God's heart. He was led to you by the Spirit of the Lord. He will bring water and you will know he is from God."

Relieved that God had shown mercy and had not exposed her sin, Mary took a deep breath, relaxed, and listened to the Lord's words through her mentor.

Quilla Mae prophesied the Lord would soon remove Mary from her position, signaling that it was time for her to launch the women's ministry. "This is the acceptable time of the Lord; He has called you for this time."

Mary inquired as to how it could be done. She lacked the funds to purchase the land, construct the structure, and provide the women with their daily necessities.

"Trust God. He will provide the Lamb. He will touch the heart of a wealthy man. He will be touched by your story, and he will give you everything you need to start debt free without finance, and the body of Christ will give lavishly to God's work," the elder replied. "They will give

CHAPTER 6

abundantly, opening their hands wide and giving daily, weekly, and monthly so that the ministry will not suffer. Jehovah Jireh will supply!"

Mary believed the words of the woman of God and went to work in peace, singing to God's abundant mercies and exceedingly abundant grace.

Before going to bed, she declared the devil a loser and began binding every spirit of darkness from entering her dreams and enticing her flesh. She went to bed confident that she would have no more dreams of sexual immortality after having the chains of masturbation severed from her.

In the early hours of the morning, the kingdom of darkness infiltrated her dreams once more with sexual perversion. The fantasy compelled her to touch herself. She felt unworthy of God's grace once more, and was angry with herself as she thought she abused His mercy.

The warfare lasted for two weeks with Mary succumbing to her flesh every night. Too embarrassed to seek the prayers of her pastor and church elders, Joshua, and Quilla Mae, she decided to confide in her best friend Luke.

They met at their favorite pizza place and ordered their usual medium cheese with peppers and olives. Mary told her friend about her recent struggles as they ate.

Luke advised that he, too, struggled with masturbation, was addicted to porn, and was promiscuous before Christ before being born again.

"The first thing you need to do is repent," Luke started calmly.

"I've asked God to take this away from me," Mary interjected, frustrated by his counsel. "I have requested the ability to resist. I apologized to God."

"Repentance does not simply mean asking for forgiveness. It also means turning away from the sin."

"That's what I'm aiming for," Mary interjected.

"Let me finish." Luke patiently lifted his hand in a gesture of peace. "Next, avoid things that can trigger you. Sexually explicit music or TV shows and movies with a lot of sexual scenes. Those triggers caused me to revert back to masturbation. Once I identified those triggers, it had a drastic effect on me.

"Third, I had a brother in Christ to hold me accountable. He prayed with me, challenged me, and chastised me. I was honest with him. When I failed, he scorned me and then built me up. As your brother in Yeshua, I will hold you accountable.

"Fourth, I had to mediate on the Word of God, because it unlocks liberation. It is through the Word that we have our liberty, and it is through Christ that we are free. As John 8:36 says, 'Therefore, if the Son makes you free, you shall be free indeed.' Every night before you go to bed, declare in the name of Jesus Christ, who the Son sets free is free indeed, and I am free from all sexual dreams, fantasies, and masturbation."

Luke promised to hold her accountable once more, and promised to pray for her every day until the lust of her flesh was gone. The two friends finished their pizza and talked about the ministry that God had placed in her heart.

When Mary returned home, she did as Luke had instructed, declaring herself free of sexual fantasies, dreams, and masturbation.

Within three hours of falling asleep, the devil began to show her sexual imagery, causing Mary's flesh to tingle. She was tempted, but instead of succumbing to her flesh, she fought to awaken.

Sitting up in her bed, she cursed the serpent and declared her victory in the name of Yeshua Hamashiach. She screamed at the top of her lungs, "I'm free of lust!" She yelled it several times, loudly and violently, to let the enemy know she meant business.

She went back to sleep. The enemy no longer attacked her dreams, and she slept peacefully for the rest of the night.

CHAPTER 6

When she awoke, she declared victory over her adversary. Giving thanks to God, she first called Luke and told him what had happened. Luke rejoiced with her in victory, but he warned her that the enemy would return and that the war was not over. He also warned her not to listen to any sexually explicit music. Mary agreed and began wearing ear plugs in the office except when speaking with her team and clients.

On Thursday night, Mary faced the devil again, proclaiming her freedom in Christ Jesus. When she awoke, her phone was ringing. Joshua was on the other line.

"For our struggle is not against flesh and blood, but against rulers, authorities, powers of this dark world, and spiritual forces of evil in the heavenly realms. By the authority given to me by Jesus Christ of Nazareth, I command that every soul tie, every covenant of darkness, and every iniquity caused by sexual immorality be broken off you in the name of Yeshua Messiah."

Even though he was not with Mary, the prophet of God, full of fire, could see what was going on in the Spirit. "2 Corinthians 10:3-4 says, 'For though we walk in the flesh, we do not war according to the flesh, For the weapons of our warfare are not carnal, but mighty in God for pulling down strongholds.' In the mighty name of Jesus Christ, I cast down every stronghold of darkness from your past!"

Mary agreed and raised her hands in solidarity as the true prophet of God continued to command darkness to flee with zeal.

"For thus said the Lord Almighty in Luke 10:19, 'I give you authority to trample on serpents and scorpions, as well as over all the power of the enemy, and nothing shall harm you.' By the blood of the Lamb and the word of your testimony, claim your victory in Jesus."

Mary followed the prophet's instructions and began to celebrate her freedom through the blood of the Lamb and the word of her testimony. She took the title of her deliverance from sexual immorality with a loud voice, declaring that she would never be enslaved by it again.

Both Mary and Joshua were overjoyed and exalted the living God, praising Him with all their might and every fiber of their being.

When the Spirit stopped moving, the prophet told her that the enemy had gained access to tempt her because of her anger and sin. While they discussed her issues with anger, the Spirit of the Lord again began to speak to His servant.

"I see water. I see you and your husband carrying water to the thirsty. You will meet him and you will know that it is him. God has ordained this union. Proverbs 11:25 says, 'The generous soul will be made rich, and he who waters will be watered himself.' The two of you will water a multitude of women. Wow, the number is so great, domestically and internationally! Start looking for a building for your ministry. God is hurrying to fulfill His word spoken over you.

Having his eyes opened by the power of God, Joshua then inquired of Mary about how things were going in the house of worship.

She told him that Pastor Peter had removed the mockers and scorners from the house of prayer, allowing her to worship in peace and serenity once more. He prophesied the members of the body of Christ would have to shut down from Sabbath to Sabbath the following Friday.

"You will hear this next Wednesday at scripture study. The under shepherd of the house will tell you what the Lion of Judah has called for. There will be an outpouring of the Holy Spirit, and all who desire Him will receive Him."

Full of revelation knowledge, Joshua knew he could continue to prophesy, but he looked at the time and realized it was 4:48 a.m. Exhausted, but content, the two wished each other peace before hanging up the phone.

Mary went to bed, and the enemy never appeared in her dreams again with sexual perversion.

***

CHAPTER 6

Wednesday came and Mary went to study God's Word with other believers of her church.

"On Monday, while praying for you all in my secret place, the Lord whispered to me, 'Shut the door.' I had no idea what that meant, so I asked, 'What does that mean?' The secret was in 2 Kings 4:33. 'He went in, shut the door behind them, and prayed to the Lord,'" Rabbi Peter told the group.

"It's the story of Elisha coming into a house and a child was lying there dead," one of the group members chimed in.

"So, what does that mean?" another member asked.

"Good question, I asked the same thing." Mary couldn't help but laugh as the other members of the group joined her. "Then I heard the words 'one accord in one place,' and it became clear to me that God desires His people to be filled with the Holy Spirit."

"I say to the Lord, when do you want to pour out your spirit on your people?" A curious woman asked.

"My spirit began to bear witness to Friday, *this* Friday. So, when the sun goes down on that day, we will be assembled in this place waiting on the precious gift of the Holy Spirit, and we will stay waiting on His manifestation until the next day, if necessary."

The small group of people were true believers in Yeshua, and they were excited for the outpouring of Mary's prophetic words, so they told all of their friends about what God would do.

On that Sabbath Friday, the faithful saints filled the house of God, their hearts overflowing with admiration, adoration, and expectation. Worshiping God in spirit and truth, they invited the presence of power to manifest Himself in all His glory.

Hundreds of people sang to him with all of their hearts, souls, and spirits. At 1:21 a.m., the God of Israel poured His Spirit on His beloved people, and a sound from heaven came as a rushing mighty wind and filled the entire house. Tongues of fire engulfed the church, and as the Holy Spirit filled them, they spoke in other tongues.

They cried tears of joy and were amazed as they celebrated God's works, saw visions, and prophesied. The glory of the Lord remained with His people as they worshiped throughout the twilight of night and the breaking of the day.

At noon, the Lord's presence was still heavy, and people on the outside in their cars saw a glowing illumination coming from the house of prayer, and they heard joyful shouts.

They parked their cars and came to investigate. The fear of the Lord overcame them, but they accepted Yeshua as Lord, and were saved and filled with the Holy Spirit.

That day, over 700 people were added to God's kingdom, many of whom came as a result of the remnant of God's glory and illumination.

Mary felt a power she had never felt before after being filled with the precious gift of the Holy Spirit. She realized the time had finally come to launch the women's ministry.

CHAPTER 7

She drove around the city for two months looking for a building and found nothing, but on the fifth day of the third month, she heard a whisper from a small still voice.

"*It's the one.*"

She got out of her car to inspect the abandoned building. It was in such disrepair and reeked of urine and feces from the homeless. Walking around the building, she realized it would be very expensive to renovate as it needed a new roof, windows, bricks, and wood for she could see termites eating it away before her eyes. For now, it was a haven for rats, spiders, raccoons, and trash. She knew she could not afford the renovation and lacked the necessary talent and labor.

"Heavenly Father," Mary prayed aloud, "are You certain this is the place for Your glory?"

She felt guilty for the doubt that had crept into her mind, yet she was answered again by the small still voice.

"*This is the one.*"

She called Luke and told him that God had given her a building, and then asked if they could meet there the following Friday. When the day arrived, Luke and Mary stood outside staring at the sad-looking building.

"We have a lot of work to do," Mary said as she shook her head, "but this is the place the Lord has chosen."

Luke crossed his arms across his chest. "This is going to take some serious resurrecting," he said as he wearily eye the decayed building, "and it's going to require a massive amount of money and love."

"I have a patient who owns a construction company. Perhaps he would be willing to give us a discount. Lord knows we certainly need it," Mary joked, but she knew Luke was correct; they needed all the help they could get. Looking at the massive project before her made her disheartened and discouraged.

Luke noticed she was becoming depressed. "Hey," he said gently as he took her hand. "If God said this is the place, He will provide the resources, and He will pay for what He orders."

Her friend's words encouraged Mary, and he suggested that they walk around the building seven times as Joshua had walked around Jericho in Joshua chapter 6. Hand in hand, the two slowly completed lap after lap. On the seventh time around, Mary was instructed by the Lord to shout loudly and claim the title deed.

Mary and Luke obeyed the Lord, and a great calm came over them. They knew they would receive the title to the building through faith when the time was right.

Over the next few weeks, she confessed daily that the building was hers. She even went so far as to tell the women at the shelter that she had a building she had called "Compassion House."

She began to write her vision and mission statement in her secret spiritual place where she prayed, fasted, and sowed. She discovered that the threefold cord of praying, fasting, and giving was not easily broken and was determined to do so for twenty-one days.

During those twenty-one days, Luke bought an engagement ring with the intention of proposing because he knew and had known for some time that Mary was his rib.

He distributed water, food, and clothing at the shelter and showed the women the engagement ring he had purchased.

CHAPTER 7

Once Mary's fasting was complete, she arrived at the Compassion House and noticed the women of the shelter were all smiling at her. Luke took advantage of the situation, got down on one knee, and asked Mary to marry him.

As he placed the ring on her finger, she immediately said yes. Mary cried tears of joy as the women surrounded the newly engaged couple, giving them hugs and well wishes. Mary had become a sister and friend to them, and now they were gaining a new brother in faith.

When the actualization began to fade, she remembered the prophecy both Quilla Mae and Joshua had told her: "you will meet him carrying water." "Meaning his generosity and charity were counted to him as righteousness" She happily kissed him again, and again, tears of joy flowed down her face.

Seeing Mary get engaged gave the ladies hope that if she could overcome the trials and tribulations she faced throughout her life, so could they; if God could do it for her, He could do it for them.

The two Christians were eager to marry because they understood exactly what God meant in I Corinthians 7:8-9. *But I say to the unmarried and to the widows: It is good for them if they remain even as I am; but if they cannot exercise self- control, let them marry. For it is better to marry than to burn with passion.*

They hadn't felt affection in years, so they planned to marry within three weeks of the proposal date.

Right on schedule on a Saturday morning, they were gathered in the house of God, and the beautiful bride stood at the altar, looking at her soon-to-be husband. The wedding was officiated by her pastor, and guests included Joshua, Quilla Mae, women from the shelter, Mary's coworkers, Luke's parents, his pastor, and his friends and colleagues.

Proverbs 18:22 was quoted by Mary's pastor to explain the joining of two fleshes as one. "'Whoever finds a wife finds a good thing and gains favor with the Lord.' In the Book of Genesis, God knew Adam could not be alone, so God took Adam's rib and made him Eve, a helper comparable to him."

When they placed the rings of unity on each other's finger and said "I do," the pastor pronounced them husband and wife. Those who witnessed the union rejoiced with the newly appointed Mr. and Mrs. Phillips and brought them gifts and adulation, calling them blessed and highly favored. The overjoyed elders encouraged them to keep Ephesians 5: 22-27, I Corinthians 7:2-5, Hebrews 13:4, Colossians 3:18, and I Peter 3:7 before their eyes

Before they left the house of the Lord, Joshua received a prompting from the Holy Spirit to bless them. He had them kneel before him as he spoke the blessing over them.

"The Lord bless you and keep you. The Lord make His face shine upon you and be gracious to you. The Lord lift up His countenance upon you, and give you peace."

God's elect stretched out their arms as the prophet poured anointing oil on their heads, prompting the elders to speak in tongues. As they spoke in their heavenly language, the prophet's eyes opened up and he saw in the Spirit a dark cloud that appeared to hinder their marriage. He blew off the dark cloud, cursing the enemy's work and rebuking his attempt to derail the marriage by concluding with Matthew 19:6, "'Therefore, what God has joined together, let not man separate.'" The black cloud receded at the light of his words as the glory of God weighted the room.

Quilla Mae received revelation from the newlyweds to take their shoes off. Luke's pastor held the anointing oil as Quilla Mae anointed their eyes to see the goodness of God, their ears to hear God's voice, and their feet to be led by God.

CHAPTER 7

That night, the couple consummated their marriage. Their undefiled bed was shared in pleasure, and the burning passion did not flame out until the next morning, almost causing them to be late for their flight.

Quilla Mae had blessed them with an all-expense-paid honeymoon trip to Paris. It was a beautiful trip where they visited museums, neighboring countries, and enjoyed art, food, fashion, and European culture.

Luke enjoyed everything about his trip to Europe, but he enjoyed practicing the Word of God more with his wife. Mary enjoyed being desired; it was a sensation she hadn't experienced in a long time, and her husband lavished her with all of the attention she required.

With great anticipation, Luke practiced what the Word said in Proverbs 5:15. *Drink water from your own cistern, and running water from your own well.* With great affection, he applied Proverbs 5:19. *As a loving deer and a graceful doe, let her breast satisfy you at all times; and always be enraptured with her love.*

They returned from their fifteen-day honeymoon spiritually, physically, and emotionally renewed. They did not waste time as both put their properties on the market. The real estate sold quickly, with Mary receiving an offer in five days and Luke receiving an offer in eight.

They purchased a home together as husband and wife. As a wedding gift, Luke's parents brought new furniture for their living and dining rooms.

Through God's wisdom, the rooms were filled with precious and pleasant riches, and the house became a sanctuary for them to worship God, enjoy each other, and start a family.

Mary was on the mountain of contentment. She had a husband who adored her, lived in a beautiful home, and was successful in her career. She was the happiest she had ever been in her life, but the call to begin the mission was constantly tugging on her heart. She had prayed for it, fasted for it, sowed for it, and even walked around it to claim the land and take the title by faith.

Mary drove to the shelter after work, her car full of Bibles, inspirational books inspired by God, clothes, food, and water. She blasted her worship music, shouting along with songs of praise. While taking the items from her trunk, she witnessed the same rapist attempt to commit an execrable crime on yet another woman.

He grabbed the woman by her hair and yelled profanity. She tried to flee, but the man was far too strong, slamming her to the ground and ripping her shirt. Mary's eyes locked with his; he recognized her. Filled with evil spirits, he screamed at Mary, his voice resembling a legion of demons, yet he did not attack her. Instead, he refocused his attention back on the young women, licked her face like a dog, and proceeded to rip her pants.

Mary quickly retrieved the pepper spray canister she kept in her glove compartment, ran over to the man, and sprayed the stinging mist directly into his eyes, He screamed in pain while swinging punches widely and blindly, hoping to make contact with his new assailant.

You will not get away this time. Your reign of terror will be over this very day, Mary thought as she continued to work quickly, guided by the Holy Spirit. Not having grabbed her phone from her car, she spied the young woman's cell phone on the ground next to the emptied contents of her purse. She picked it up, dialed 911, and relayed just enough information to the cops to know what was happening and where the attack was occurring.

The stocky assailant went back and forth, unsure of where the women were to attack or where an escape route could be. Unsure how long the pepper spray would work on this monster, Mary half-handed, half-dropped the cell phone into the young woman's lap, the cops still on the phone, then leapt on the assailant's back. The man did not expect the attack and both he and Mary fell to the ground. The fall was harsh enough to stun them both, but Mary would not allow him to get away. Planting her body weight firmly on his torso, she wrapped her arms around his

CHAPTER 7

and held him in a position where he could not move easily. She refused to move until she heard the glorious sound of sirens heading their way.

Within minutes of the call, the police assigned to that jurisdiction arrived. They ran to the young woman's aid, still sitting on the ground clutching her cell phone, and apprehended the rapist, ensuring Mary was not hurt as they helped her release her hold of him.

Mary tried to calm the young women down as the officers took their statements, but the victim's emotions could not be tamed. This invidious assault was too much for her to bear and the traumatic experience had numbed her. Instead of going to the hospital and police station, she wanted nothing more than to go home.

Mary consoled and prayed for the young lady until her parents arrived. The mother and father thanked and praised Mary endlessly before driving away.

Mary, still fuming over the incident, delivered the materials to the women at the shelter, but she didn't stay long. She drove home in a frenzy, thinking about the woman she had just saved from depression, dread, and perhaps hypersexuality. The more she thought about the psychological and emotional scaring that poor woman would not go through, the angrier she became. She began to remember her attacks and her attacker.

When she got home, her husband could tell by the look on her face that movie night would have to wait, and readied himself to play counselor.

"Monday morning, I'm going to the tax assessor's office to find out who owns that dilapidated building, and I'm going to buy it! I know I don't have the money to restore it, but I'll use the proceeds from the condo sale. I'll get a loan, I'll seek private funding, I'll do whatever I have to do, but I'm tired of waiting! There are women out there who are hurting, confused, and in danger. Now is the time to do what God has ordained. Now is the time to obey God."

CHANGING FILTHY GARMENTS

Luke tried to soothe his wife's distress, but she refused. The third attack from the same assailant had lit a fire under her for the entire weekend. While the vile man she had seen was now finally apprehended, she could only wonder how many more women would be hurt from other lustful men...

She went into her boss's office on Monday and put her resignation on his desk. He assumed it was a joke, but Mary assured him it wasn't. He begged her not to for everything was going so well in her life and there were so many reasons not to quit.

Mary insisted that her decision was final and that she had to follow God's instructions. After much resistance, her manager finally accepted the letter. He was saddened and knew she would be sorely missed, so he gave her a compassionate hug and told her to inform her team and clients.

When she shut the door, a spirit of trepidation tried to overshadow her; it would be the first time in her adult life that she would have to rely on someone else for income.

She cast the fear out and wiped away her tears. She called her staff and broke the news to them. They all bowed their heads in sorrow, though some hoped it was a joke. Mary's voice cracked as she told them how much she loved them and thanked them for their work.

Their tears made Mary cry for they had become her family as well as her friends. No one under her supervision wanted her to leave. They hugged her constantly as she told them about the journey she had to take.

She interrupted the sobbing to inform the clients she was onboarding that her lead would be handling their account in her absence.

Clients were as surprised as her coworkers. They didn't want her to leave for she had brought them so much success. Many of her clients sent flowers, candy, cards, and their best wishes after hearing the news.

CHAPTER 7

She left work early to inquire about who owned the property. After the tax assessor looked through the many files, she was given the name and number of the property owner as well as a forwarding address in South Dakota.

When she returned home, she informed her husband that she had indeed resigned and that she had obtained the information from the property owner. She dialed the number, but the line was disconnected, so she wrote to the address on file, hoping to hear back within a few days.

CHAPTER 8

Mary and Luke did not hear from the owner of the property for weeks. They began to worry maybe he was dead and they would have to find his relatives, which could take forever. She started to question her timing for the decision to quit her career.

The next month, a letter from a man named George Bonds came to the mailbox. He'd received their letter and was willing to sell them the property for two million dollars.

The newlyweds were flabbergasted and discouraged. They didn't have two million dollars! Luke suggested they get a loan and sell their new home, and Mary was all too willing to follow her husband; however, after a moment of calm and clarity, she remembered the prophecies of Quilla Mae and Joshua: they would not need a loan or government assistance.

She called Joshua and Quilla Mae on conference to seek their counsel. Quilla Mae answered with God's Word, as she often did, quoting Deuteronomy 6:10-11. "'So it shall be when the Lord your God brings you into the land of which He swore to your fathers, to Abraham, Isaac, and Jacob, to give you large and beautiful cities which you did not fill, hewn out wells which you did not dig, vineyards and olives trees which you did not plant.'"

"He is going to give it you! Go to the building and start to clean. When you start moving, God will start moving," Joshua echoed Quilla Mae's sentiments. "Instructions always precede a miracle."

The words encouraged Luke and his wife. Mary intended to do just as the woman and man of God had said.

On Monday morning, Mary rose up early as if she were going to work, but instead of putting on a business suit and heels, she wore an old t-shirt, an old pair of jeans, and scuffed up boots. She thought she was crazy by cleaning up a property that did not belong to her, but she obeyed the Word of the Lord.

On the fifteenth day of faithfully going what she continued to call "Compassion House," Luke and Mary were working hard when someone stopped by. A man stepped out of his luxury vehicle accompanied by two other men. Mary wiped the sweat from her brow as she walked toward the three. As she got closer, she recognized Tom Moore, the marketing director of an account she had handled for years at her previous job.

"It's great to see you, Tom." Mary smiled as she shook his hand. "To what do I owe the pleasure of your visit?"

"It is good to see you, too, Mary. This is Andrew David, my boss and the owner of the many products that you advertised. And this is his personal assistant, Alex Miller." Mary shook hands with each of the men as they were introduced.

"Mrs. Phillips, I've heard nothing but good things about you from Tom," Mr. David said. "Our products performed admirably during your time at the station."

Mary couldn't help but smile at the wealthy man's praise.

"I was concerned when Tom told me you were leaving. I assumed you were going to another company and that I should hire you myself," he continued, "but when he told me that you were starting this, I became even more impressed with you and wanted to know your story.

"Like you, my daughter was raped, and my wife and I spent thousands of dollars on therapists, counselors, medications, and facilities, but she was still unable to recover from the trauma and evil

CHAPTER 8

thoughts. It wasn't until someone introduced her to Jesus that she was set free and healed, and with that healing, she no longer required anti-depressant medications. She stopped seeing therapists and counselors, testifying that Yeshua Hamashiach had healed her. Her zeal and passion won me over, and I began to reconsider my life, my wealth, my legacy, what I was doing, and what it all meant.

"So, I no longer put my trust in uncertain riches, and Mark 10:25 no longer applies to me. Instead, I stand on 1 Timothy 6:17, 'Command those who are wealthy in this day and age not to be arrogant, nor to put their trust in uncertain riches, but in the living God, who lavishes us with all things to enjoy.' I was so preoccupied with making money that I had little time for my family, especially my daughter! I would run after money, but now it runs after me. So now, instead of squandering my wealth on frivolous purchases, I use it to fund projects like this."

With that, his assistant handed over an envelope, and the three walked away without another word. The chauffeur opened the door for them, and Mary and Luke waved goodbye as they drove away.

Mary's hands were sweaty as she held the envelope. She was too scared to open it, but Luke urged her to take a deep breath and go for it. She fumbled and dropped it once to the ground. When she picked it up, she carefully tore the corners off and opened it.

She was taken aback by the amount of money the generous Christian believer had given her. The check read "five million dollars," more than enough to buy, repair, and staff Compassion House! She screamed and covered her mouth as tears streamed down her checks. She handed the check to her husband and began to praise God for His faithfulness! Jehovah Jireh had provided far more than He had promised!

The Phillips gave Him the fruit of their lips in praise. Luke, amazed, continued to stare at the five million dollar check. He hugged his wife, overwhelmed. They smiled and hugged each other continuously.

What Ephesians 3:20 said was true! It had come true in their life!

When they walked out in faith, they were met with Adonai's supernatural abundance, but the God who gives good gifts to His children kept adding to His impeccable reputation with this miracle of grace.

They couldn't finish the day as they were too excited and wished to share the good news. They called Quilla Mae, Joshua, and the rest of their *mishpachah* to tell them about the wonderful thing the Lord had done. Luke called his client who owned a construction company and they agreed to meet Monday morning.

The Phillips were the first people at the bank on Monday. Once the funds were deposited, they wired two million dollars to the owner of the abandoned building. Mr. Bonds provided them with a bill of sale indicating that the property had been paid in full and was now theirs.

Mary and Luke went to their new property and walked around it with Dan Miller the owner of the construction company. He gave the Phillips a rough estimate of the property according to Mary's vision, and she believed that anything bearing the name of God should be glorious and exceptional.

Dan wanted the house that would bear the Lord's name to be magnificent, as well, so he promised to use only the best materials and people. They finalized the paperwork on Thursday after a thorough review of the cost, which came in at around 1.5 million dollars with all of the specifications and upgrades. Mary signed the contract with her husband standing right at her side.

Monday morning, Dan and a crew of twelve began work on Compassion House. He estimated that the project would be completed by December 28, allowing them to accept women at the start of the new year.

CHAPTER 9

On January 8 the following year, Mary and Luke cut the ribbon on the fully renovated building, which brimmed with splendor. The very best people were hired, and every member of the staff was born again. They included therapists, counselors, life coaches, teachers, pastors, cooks, and housekeepers. When God's elect were ready to serve and were placed on salary, they opened the door to women who had been raped, addicted, rejected, heavy laden, poor in spirit, and unwanted.

The women came in droves, many from the shelter Mary served at. She was overjoyed for within three months of opening Compassion House, it was filled to capacity, hosting 180 women. God was faithful to heal the women of their painful trauma through the faithful witness of the staff and souls were won for the kingdom of God. Nothing could compare to seeing women freed from bondage, their spirits transferred from darkness to light.

By God's grace, old things had passed away, and all things were made new. As Romans 10:9 said, *They confessed the Lord Jesus with their mouths and believed in their hearts that God raised Him from the dead, and they were saved.* It was true; it was glorious! Alive! Anew! They basked in new life and endless possibilities.

The women were no longer slaves of sin as they walked as light in the newness of life, laying aside every weight. For some it was alcoholism, for others it was drugs, and for many it was sin of fornication.

Regardless of the yoke that had enslaved them, those who received Yeshua were set free by the blood of the Lamb. For months to come, the glory of God rested on Compassion House. Women came in tormented, bound, and low, and were introduced to the love of Christ. They confessed their sins and received His salvation through His blood. They left in freedom, with no chains left to hold them, and they soared as eagles.

It was harvest time, souls and hearts were being filled with the hope of glory. Mary and the staff rejoiced over the salvations that occurred. For the entire year, there was peace and joy as God performed significant miracles.

**

The following year began just as the previous one had ended. Women came to Compassion House seeking relief from the chains of rape, sexual assault, and sexual abuse. Their troubled souls required a cure, so the staff introduced that cure: Jesus the Christ, the Son of God. He was more than willing to heal them.

Those who received His healing were healed, but in the second half of the year, Mary and her staff were confronted with a spirit of confusion sent by the enemy. A foe that Mary was all too familiar with… and one she thought had been defeated, but who had reappeared.

A small group of women refused to submit to Yeshua Hamashiach's lordship. They did not adhere to God's laws, listen to, or respect the leadership placed over them. Mary tried to persuade them, but the rebellious women refused to change their ways.

CHAPTER 9

Mary had been successful in converting other women to the knowledge of Christ, His crucified body to heal their scars of emotional, psychological, and physical abuse. She assumed these women would be no different. They were just as hardheaded as she had been for so many years, so she gave them more time as God had given her.

She earnestly stood on the wall for them, pleading with God to heal them of all their pain and trauma, but the women refused her prayers, openly rebelling and creating an atmosphere of hostility, confusion, and anger.

These indignant women filled with lust and a hypersexual appetite invited men and women in the middle of the night into Compassion House. They entered with alcohol, marijuana, and cocaine. When Mary learned of this, she became enraged and confronted them, yelling at them for desecrating the Lord's house with drugs and sexual perversion.

Three of the six women yelled back at her. Mary physically fought back with rage, giving one of them a black eye, the other a busted lip, and the third a cut in the face. When the police arrived, all six women, including Mary, were arrested, and because it was late on a Friday, they were detained for the entire weekend.

Monday morning, Luke arrived at the jail to pick up his wife. He was so disappointed in her for allowing anger to get the best of her yet again. He chastised her on the way home, but Mary was still angry and yelled at him. The two screamed at each other the entire ride home.

Tuesday morning, the story made front-page news for local stations. It was all over the internet and went viral on social media websites, spreading like wildfire as those who despised Yeshua plastered it everywhere.

Mary was mocked as a hypocrite. They questioned her transformation and dug deep into her past, highlighting her career in pornography. They questioned how God could use such a person and demanded her entire operation to be shut down, labeling it a scam aimed at robbing people of their money.

For weeks, the press reported Compassion House woes, and those infused with the spirit of the Antichrist opposed anything that reflected Christ's character. Those who hated Christians shared it on their television stations, newspapers, and social media platforms aimed to discredit her, her passion, and the name of Jesus.

This hurt Mary more than being raped. She was harassed by reporters and freelancers for weeks. She did finally manage to elude the press, yet people in the grocery store, at the hairdresser, or other stores while she ran errands looked at her with disdain and made horrifying remarks. It was the looks of shame and disgust she had received from the Pharisees. Her house was just as cold on the inside as it was on the outside, filled with frustration, irritability, and anger.

She was once in a season of spring and blossom, but winter had returned, and it was bitterly cold. Her ministry, once filled, was now at half-staff as Mary had been forced to reduce more staff. The enemy was winning… Her name had been shamed, her ministry was in jeopardy, her marriage was rocky, she was depressed, and the Lord's mouth was closed.

She was mad at Him; she needed a sign, a prompting, a word, anything, but God refused to speak. Months passed and nothing encouraging happened. Mary sulked in her house until she received a call from Joshua. Recognizing his number, she smiled. Surely the Lord had given him a word for her. She picked up the phone on the first ring and expected him to start speaking in an unknown tongue, but he did not. They talked for thirty minutes with no word of knowledge.

As the conversation fizzled, Joshua gave her incite for the resolution she desired. "The solution to your problem is in your husband's hands. He is a wise man of God, and Yahweh has given him the answer to turn your situation around."

CHAPTER 9

They hung up the phone after bidding each other *shalom*. There was no prophecy, no speaking in tongues, no word of knowledge. Mary humbled herself in order to follow the prophet's advice. She knocked on the guest bedroom door where her husband had been sleeping for far too long. Luke welcomed her in and sat on the edge of the bed. After thirty seconds of awkward silence, Mary closed her eyes, hung her head, and muttered, "I'm sorry Luke." A tear rolled down her left cheek, followed by her right.

Luke turned to his wife beside him and hugged her. He expressed his sorrow and asked to be forgiven. The two forgave each other and continued to sit on the bed together even after they had parted from their embrace.

"Go back to Georgia. You need to forgive your mother and the man who raped you," Luke said. "It's the only way to be completely free, the only way to be completely healed."

Mary followed her husband's advice and purchased a ticket to fly into Savannah the following Monday.

Sunday night at 3:23 a.m., the word of the Lord made flesh manifested Himself to Mary. She immediately recognized Him as Jesus of Nazareth, the hope of glory. She felt unworthy and began to repent. His face was filled with light, and the warmth of His grace and mercy seemed tangible.

He quoted Revelation 1:8 to her. "'*I am the Alpha and the Omega, the beginning and the end, who is and who was, and who is to come, the Almighty.*'"

His voice was like the sound of many waters flowing through her, and she could feel love emanating from Him. She was terrified, but the Prince of Peace recited Revlation 1:17-18.

"'*Do not be afraid; I am the first and the Last. I am He who lives, and was dead, and behold, I am alive forevermore.*'"

The Holy One reached out His hand toward Mary and continued quoting from the Book of Revelation, verse 3:5 this time. "'*Hold fast and repent walk with Me in white, He who overcomes shall be clothed in white garments, and I will not blot out his name from the book of life, but I will confess his name before My Father and before His angels.'*

"Refrain from anger; don't let your spirit be quick to become angry. Forgive, and you will be forgiven. Forgive them so that your Heavenly Father may forgive your sins."

Hearing the Word of Yeshua, she began to cry. Her husband's words had been confirmed, and she needed to forgive her mother and her rapist. She placed her right hand in the Master's right hand, and her burdens were lifted. Worrying stopped as a love she couldn't explain overwhelmed her. God's love transformed her anger into love beyond comprehension. He smiled and said before leaving.

"Says Revelation 3:20-21, 'If anyone hears My voice and opens the door, I will come in to him and with him and he with me. To him who overcomes I will grant to sit with me on My throne, as I also overcome and sat down with My Father on His throne.'"

Mary awoke to see her hand outstretched as if she was still holding the hand of Jesus. She thanked the Lord as she cried tears of joy. Luke awoke to find his wife crying and her face glowing with the glory of God. She told him of her encounter with the King of Kings and Lord of Lords

She flew into Savannah early the next morning and then drove to Baxley. She stopped by Quilla Mae's ranch and told her about her encounter with Yeshua Hamashiach. The elder listened intently and recalled her previous encounters with Jesus Christ.

Mary spent the next few days walking the large acre ranch with her spiritual mentor, partaking in the activities she loved to do when was growing up and seeing people she hadn't seen in over twenty years.

As she sat on the porch drinking sweet tea one morning, she realized how much she had missed the slow southern pace. It was refreshing after the hustle and bustle of Los Angeles.

CHAPTER 9

Amanda no longer lived in her trailer, and was now in a drug rehab facility. On Friday, Mary traveled to the facility, knowing that seeing her biological mother would bring back feelings of abandonment, deprotection, and anger, but she persisted. She needed to look her mother in the eye and say, "I forgive you."

She sat quietly and anxiously as the guard went to retrieve her mother. As she waited patiently, she wrestled with many emotions until her mother appeared. A daze came over her as she had not seen the woman who birthed her in over twenty years. Strange enough, her mother reached out to give her a hug, which made Mary feel awkward.

She couldn't help but notice the harsh effects of time, substance abuse, and prostitution on her as she appeared older than any woman her age should look. She had no teeth, there were patches on her face, and most of her hair had fallen out. Mary could barely recognize the women who bore her.

Mary asked her to sit, and they both unconsciously agreed to start small talk before sparring. The easy and non-combative conversation lasted forty minutes, but it gradually shifted from rhetorical and informative questions when Mary simply had to ask, "Did you know?"

Amanda lowered her head and began to cry. It wasn't a joyful cry like when her daughter called to say she wanted to see her or the tears shed when she embraced her. These were tears of shame, the shame of a mother who allowed her daughter to be raped repeatedly by a violent criminal. With remorse, she confirmed Mary's suspicions.

Mary felt her heart fill with rage. She wanted to lash out. She wanted to demand what mother would allow her daughter, her only child, to be knowingly violated.

"I'm sorry! I'm so sorry! Please, forgive me! Please, have mercy on me!" Amanda begged.

The more she begged for mercy, the more enraged Mary became. How could she know and not intervene? What kind of mother was she? Mary was about to explode when she heard a still small voice speak to her.

"Blessed are the merciful, for they shall receive mercy. Be merciful, just as your Father is merciful. Forgive, and you shall be forgiven."

Mary remembered her Savior's dream and heeded His words. She cast her anger into the pits of hell from which it had come, grabbed her mother's hands, and said, "I apologize. You are forgiven."

Amanda wept as she finally gained her daughter's forgiveness for the negligence she had shown in her motherhood. The more she cried, the burden she had carried for so many years was lifted from her soul. Dejected for so many years, she was able to breathe easily after being granted mercy.

Mary wiped Amanda's tears from her eyes. "Now I want you to forgive yourself," Mary told her mother after going through the process of self-hatred. "God will forgive you, but you must learn to forgive yourself."

Amanda wrapped her arms around her daughter, and the embrace was therapeutic for both of them. Amanda sighed, as if she could breathe again, the colossal weight of shame and humiliation obliterated by the power of grace and mercy. She then begged God to forgive her for her sins after hearing about His power to remove sin, shame, and addiction.

With her mother's chains removed, Mary took advantage of the opportunity to bear witness to Yeshua, the light of the world. She placed her hands on her mother's forehead and prayed to God to remove her addiction.

"There is no one like You in heaven or on Earth, Heavenly Father. You are the God of Gods. Nothing is too difficult for You. With You, all things are possible! Father, in the name of Your

CHAPTER 9

only Begotten Son, Jesus the Messiah, remove the curse of drugs from this woman's life. Cast this demon into the lake of fire; it shall no longer torment her. She is free in the name of Jesus!"

Amanda instantly felt the craving, desire, and taste for drugs flee from her. She shouted for joy, knowing she had been delivered that very moment. Mary praised God with her, having experienced the power of God's deliverance herself. Amanda desired Yeshua to be Lord over her life, so her daughter led her in a repentance prayer. She confessed her sins and acknowledged Jesus as her Lord. The precious blood of the Lamb saved the life that the devil wanted to destroy, and the sisters in Christ hugged and celebrated Amanda's new citizenship in the kingdom of God.

"'When the enemy shall come in like a flood, the Spirit of the Lord shall lift up a standard against him,'" Mary, the new elder in the Lord, warned her through Isaiah 59:19. "The enemy will try to make you remember your past, make you feel unworthy of God's grace. He will try to crush you with shame; don't fall prey to his tricks. God's grace is sufficient. God's mercy endures forever, and whoever the Son sets free is free indeed!"

Mary pulled her Bible out of her purse and read Romans 8:1. "'There is therefore now no condemnation to those who are in Christ Jesus, who do not walk according to the flesh, but according to the Spirit.'" She then turned to Psalm 103:12. "'As far as the east is from the west so far has He removed our transgressions from us.'" She finished by reading Hebrews 8:12. "'For I will be merciful to their unrighteousness, their sins and their laws deeds I will remember no more.'"

Mary paused to close her Bible before looking her mother in the eye. "You must be rooted in God's Word. Satan will remind you of your sin and shame when he does. Tell him the scapegoat has taken it away and chooses not to remember it anymore."

Amanda was given a pen and paper by the security officer, and she wrote down everything her daughter had said. The children of God talked freely as mother and daughter, the conversation filled with love, peace, and encouragement.

Before leaving, Mary and her mother requested a weekend pass so Amanda could be baptized in Tybee Island's ocean waters. The supervisor approved and granted Amanda permission.

Quilla Mae, Amanda, and Mary drove to Savannah to baptize the new Christian convert. They baptized Amanda in the name of the Father, Son, and Holy Spirit.

Before returning to Baxley, the ladies basked in the sun and told fond stories about Lois and how much they truly missed her. The three women went to the Lord's house on Sunday morning. Some people remembered Mary's days in pornography and greeted her with disdain, but they only knew of the Mary before Christ, not the Mary after Christ.

Mary had received those looks before and was used to them, but her mother, a new creation, was surprised. She had received them in the world while addicted, but she couldn't believe it also happened in God's house.

Mary revealed the secret to getting over their dirty and judgmental looks. "Smile, laugh, and respond with the Lord's Word in Psalm 107:2. 'Let the Lord's redeemed say so, who He has redeemed from the hand of the enemy.' When they look at you with shame and contempt, look them in the eyes and say, 'So? I have been redeemed by the blood of the Lamb.'"

Amanda laughed, appreciating the advice. She would certainly need it. Sitting in the third pew, the three women enjoyed the worship service and the pastor's message of the grace and mercy of a loving savior.

When he finished preaching, sinners came forward to repent and ask Jesus to be Lord over them. The pastor led the sinners to the Great Shepherd, and a dozen people accepted Yeshua as Lord.

After Mary spoke with old classmates and hugged friendly faces, she invited friends to Quilla Mae's house. Her spiritual mentor cooked for them all, and it was the best food Mary had tasted in twenty years.

CHAPTER 9

The ladies sat on the porch overlooking the well-kept lawn, completely satisfied. Amanda didn't want to leave for she thoroughly enjoyed spending time with her daughter and Quilla Mae, but she had to go back. Mary vowed to keep in touch.

Monday, Tuesday, and Wednesday, Mary continued to reconnect with all of her friends. They went to restaurants, went shopping, and talked about their lives. Some were married, some divorced, some had older children, some were new mothers, some were entrepreneurs, some had full-time careers, and some had part-time jobs.

Holding the babies of her friends made Mary long for one of her own. Being married to a godly man and being born again changed her perspective on life. Before, she never wanted to bring children into the world for she believed it was too dark, knowing first-hand how the devil could use malice and abomination to destroy destinies. But being alive unto Jehovah and holding newborns and seeing toddlers touched her heart. She knew it was God's will for her to procreate with her husband.

Her time in Georgia had been successful so far. Her mother had found salvation through Yeshua, old relationships had been reestablished, and she now desired children. The final hurdle was an hour away… in prison. The night before, as she lay in bed, looking out the window at the hundred-plus acre ranch, she prayed for strength to confront her violator.

She pondered how her life would have turned out if the initial rape had never occurred. Would she still be running? Would she be an Olympian with a gold medal? Would she be Mary of Compassion House if she wasn't raped? One thing that she did know, what the devil meant for evil, God had turned around for good. Because of God's grace, she was ministering to women from all walks of life—different colors, ethnicities, values, and cultures—and because of His grace, she shared the gospel of Jesus Christ with all of them.

Perhaps the rapist had something to do with it, but he also caused her shame, hypersexuality, and battles with dark spirits of anger, depression, loneliness, unworthiness, and disgrace. Many scenarios ran through her mind before she was able to relax and ask the Lord's grace and mercy to be with her tomorrow.

The sun pierced through the blinds. She could hear the horse galloping, meaning her mentor was up early riding. She opened the window, the brisk wind gently touching her skin as if the Son of righteousness was favoring her that day. As she basked in the glory of the Lord, the breeze flowed through her hair, signaling a flow of the Spirit.

She jumped in the shower, brushed her teeth, and dressed herself, ready to finish what she had come to do. Quilla Mae met her at the car, anointed her head with olive oil, and prayed for the man who had raped her to be released from the prayers she had prayed years before. She declared victory over Mary, the battle already won by Yeshua the Messiah.

When she arrived at the prison and signed in, Mary went to the visitor's section to await Talmai. He was serving a thirty-year sentence for drug possession, drug trafficking, burglary, rape, and sodomy; however, security officers from the prison's hospice division were dispatched to retrieve him. He would not complete that sentence as he did not have long to live.

As Mary waited, she thought about where God had brought her and began to smile just as they rolled Talmai out. Her heart dropped, her smile straightened, and she took a deep breath. It was a sobering moment as the officers and nurses retreated back to allow them to speak privately.

With him in front of her eyes, her palms began to sweat. She found herself hyperventilating. To calm herself, she whispered Psalm 46:1. "'God is my refuse and strength a very present help in trouble.'" This scripture had helped her many times before; she needed it to be true again.

With her composure somewhat restored, Mary looked at Talmai, once big and strong, now shriveled, feeble, weak, and sickly looking as he moved gingerly in his wheelchair. Mary could see why he was in hospice; the medical staff had given him a week to live, but Mary wondered if he could make it that long as his face was sucked in, his bones popping out through his frail skin.

He was not the man who raped her. That man was strong and violent; this man she could push over with one finger. Expecting the spirit of anger and rage to come over here, she looked on him with compassion and pity instead.

"Do you remember me?" she asked with a proud voice, no longer a victim of the devil's work.

"Yes, Mary. I remember you," the meager man hooked up to various tubes and an oxygen machine replied faintly.

"Do you remember what you did to me?" she inquired.

Talmai, half-dead, answered faintly, "I remember." He dropped his head in shame. Every move seemed to take an exorbitant amount of energy. He expected to be cursed and even assaulted, but was surprised by Mary's words.

"I came here to forgive you," Mary began slowly, but with conviction. "I forgave my mother, and now I have come to forgive you. I've lived with this burden and its consequences for far too long. It has taken me to places I should not have gone. It has caused me to live in a state of rage, anger, and fear, but the only cure for these diseases is forgiveness. So, I've returned home to say, no more bondage, no more enslavement. I forgive you."

The rapist was taken aback. He had not expected to be forgiven. "I'm so sorry. I have hurt so many people in my life," he sniffled, wiping the tears from his eyes, the very act exhausting him. "I have not lived a very good life. I have hurt people, and now my life is over." Weeping from the pain he had caused others, the nurse came over to offer him comfort and affix his mask and tubes in his arms.

Though she had every right to be angry with him, Mary pitied him. He'd done nothing good in his life but evil, and as she looked on him with compassion, she could see worms inside his body eating his flesh. She immediately remembered the Lord's Word in Acts 12:23. *Then immediately an angel of the Lord struck him, because he did not give glory to God, and he was eaten by worms and died.*

Sympathy filled Mary's heart. He'd allowed the devil to use him his entire life. The man she'd dreamed of killing many times was now nothing more than a walking skeleton destined to die a premature death with sickness and disease.

Her compunction assured she could see Adonai's wrath for wronging His children. The Lord's word was fulfilled in Romans 12:19. *Beloved, do not avenge yourselves, but rather give place to wrath; for it is written, vengeance is Mine, I will repay, says the Lord.*

It was all happening right in front of her eyes, and she was terrified. She could see the consequences of falling into the hands of the living God.

In the midst of her daze, she was compelled to pray for him. Surely, he was on his way to hell, a place of weeping and gnashing of teeth. A place of darkness where the spirit would never find rest and forever be tormented. A lake of fire that would never be quenched.

A man who had wounded her spiritually, emotionally, psychologically, and physically, a man she wanted to kill, a man she wanted to go to hell, was now before her, and she felt compelled to pray for him and lead him to Christ. She paused and thanked God in her mind for it could only be His doing.

Grabbing his hand again, she told him she had forgiven him and asked if he wanted to accept Jesus into his heart and live with Him in paradise.

"I've made far too many mistakes... I have hurt many people... Surely God does not want me..." he said, exhausted from speaking. The nurse gave him water as he had begun to cry again, recalling his horrifying past.

CHAPTER 9

"I forgive you," Mary said again. "God will forgive you, as well, if you repent of your sins and invite Him into your heart." He was hesitant, propped up by the nurse, he couldn't believe the Lord would forgive someone like him.

Mary released Talmai's hands so she could take out her small pocket Bible and led him to Luke 23. She expounded on the thief on the cross with Yeshua and read verse 43 aloud to him. "'And Jesus said to him, assuredly, I say to you today, you will be with Me in Paradise.'"

Talmai heard, but it didn't sink in that God would forgive him for all of the wrongs and devious acts he had committed.

Mary took his hand in hers once more and said to him, "I forgive you for what you did to me."

Something about Mary saying she forgave him for the third time struck a chord with the former rapist. As he struggled to sit up in his wheelchair, he wondered if God could give her the strength, the courage, the grace to forgive him, maybe this God could truly forgive him of all his trespasses against His creation.

Mary could see the dying man wanted to believe the Lamb of God made atonement by the shedding of His blood for all including him, but he wrestled with the sins of his past. He questioned if he could be saved. Mary assured him he could. She read Romans 6:23 to him. "For the wages of sin is death, but God's gift is eternal life through Christ Jesus our Lord."

She then read Ephesians 1:7 as Talmai became more receptive. "'Through His blood, we have redemption, and the forgiveness of sins according to the riches of His grace.'"

After seeing and hearing the Word of God read to him, the decrepit sinner began to reason with himself that perhaps God could forgive him of his sins, but he wanted to hear Mary say to him again that she had forgiven him one more time.

Mary stood up from her chair, closed the gap between them, bent down, and hugged the man who had once tormented her constantly. When she let go of him, she grabbed his skinny, scrawny arms, his shoulders so frail she could break them. Looking him in the eye, she said one more time, "I forgive you."

It was the fourth time Mary said those words, the last time very convincingly. It finally hit him. The once drug dealer, drug addict, thief, robber, and rapist had been forgiven by his victim because of the scriptures she read.

Mary verbally led him in repentance of sins, citing Romans 10:9. "'That if you confess with your mouth the Lord Jesus and believe in your heart that God has raised Him from the dead, you will be saved.'"

Talmai confessed Jesus as Lord with his mouth and finally believed in his heart. He was no longer destined for hell's fire and the brimstone of its fury.

He could look forward to being in paradise with a compassionate God. His name written in the Lamb's Book of Life.

Before Mary departed, Talmai tried to rise to his feet with his last remaining strength, but he was too weak and had to be assisted by the nurses. On his feet, he hugged the woman he had caused so much pain, and they cried in each other's arms, both experiencing freedom, one from the execution of sin and the other from the incumbrance of that sin.

Walking out of the prison, Mary felt as if she were walking on air. Lightness and freshness were her portion, her spirit soared as an eagle, just as it did when she first received Yeshua many years ago.

She lifted her voice and praised the Most High God in the car. She'd forgiven her abuser, and God had granted her the grace to lead his soul to Christ. She heard a voice say, "*Well done,*" as she euphorically gave the King the fruit of her lips for what He had done.

When Mary arrived at her spiritual mentor's house, Quilla Mae was feeding the horses in the stables. Mary ran to her arms, hugged her, and told her everything the Lord had done. Quilla Mae rejoiced with her, thanking God that the boulder that had weighed her spiritual daughter down for so long had been removed.

Quilla Mae awoke on Monday morning and prepared a hearty breakfast for Mary before her flight back to Los Angeles. She served scrambled eggs, turkey bacon, oatmeal, French toast, and fruit. They discussed Mary's victorious trip, praising God for all of the baggage that had been dumped and the relationships that had been restored.

After breakfast, Mary finished packing while promising her spiritual mentor that she would return home three times a year to see her and Amanda.

Quilla Mae received a call shortly before Mary left… Talmai had passed away during the night. Mary couldn't help but smile when she heard the news. God had used her to snare a soul destined for hell, and with His grace, she had ushered the former rapist into the presence of the Lord.

The ladies were overjoyed in the car. God was so gracious 2 Peter 3:9 was true. *The Lord is not slack concerning His promise, as some count slackness, but is longsuffering toward us, not willing that should perish but that all should come to repentance.*

The man had not died; he was on his way to the New Jerusalem. Mary continued to smile as she imagined what it would be like. Quilla Mae stated that she would see His face every day and worship Him.

As Quilla Mae read the words from the Book of Revelation, their minds raced with the imagery. Revelation 21:11 said, "'Her light was like a most precious stone, like a jasper stone, clear as crystal.'"

Oh, what a great city they discussed as they continued to Revelation 21:18-20! "'The construction of its wall was jasper; and the city was pure gold like clear glass. Jasper, sapphire, chalcedony, emerald, sardonyx, sardius, chrysolite, beryl, topaz, chrysoprase, jacinth, amethyst, pearls, the street of the city was pure gold, like transparent glass.'"

CHANGING FILTHY GARMENTS

"Oh, what a God, what a Father, what a King!" Quilla Mae exclaimed as she continued reading while Mary drove.

The two women were overjoyed about their inheritance. Quilla Mae smiled, her spirit leaping inside her with excitement and anticipation. They prayed to the Holy One of Israel to have their names written in the Book of Life.

Mary did not want to get out of the car she was so happy, but she needed to get back to her husband and the women at Compassion House. She hugged the woman she referred to as her spiritual mother and returned home.

***

Her husband picked her up from the airport and kissed her repeatedly. They were so happy to see each other. It was true that absence did make the heart grow fonder. Holding hands on the way home, Mary told Luke about all the Lord's wonders she had witnessed in Georgia.

Luke was overjoyed as Mary was joyful and pleasant to be around once more. This was his desire for his wife, a life free of fury and rage. He, unfortunately, did have bad news to share, but he didn't want to upset her or ruin their reunion.

When they arrived home, Luke had roses and chocolates waiting on the kitchen counter. He kissed his wife passionately. It was the longest time they had ever been apart since their marriage. To set the ambience for love, Mary could faintly hear soft music coming from their bedroom.

The two shared a strawberry from mouth to mouth, then Luke quickly lifted Mary into his arms and walked her down the hall. Slow jazz played as they reached the bedroom. Luke laid Mary on a bed covered with roses. The husband and wife undefiled bed burned with desired passions until the sun peaked into their window shade.

CHAPTER 9

Mary got up the next morning to make her husband breakfast. Luke smelled the pleasant aroma and was thankful his wife was home. She made his favorite: freshly squeezed orange juice, French toast with extra cinnamon, cheese eggs, turkey sausage, and potatoes.

They told each other how much they loved each other and how the time apart had helped them. They apologized to one another and promised to use the proper tone when speaking to each other. When they disagreed, Mary promised to practice Proverbs 15:1, Proverbs 16:24, and Proverbs 25:11.

Luke could see his wife was renewed and her spirit was uncluttered. He didn't want to ruin the mood, but he had to deliver the bad news.

"Do you remember the fight with the ladies from Compassion House?" he asked when they had sat down to eat.

Mary shrugged her shoulders and nodded.

"Well, those ladies are suing us. We have to appear in court next Friday. They have hired one of the best lawyers in Los Angeles, Ethan Grant. He's a crusader for atheist causes, despises Christians, and is regarded as the architect of the antichrist legal counsel in Los Angeles. He not only wants to take everything we have; he wants to shut down Compassion House."

When Luke told Mary the news, he expected her to go into a rage, lashing out with a fiery tirade, but she did not become depressed nor did she go into a tirade or swear. Instead, she began to laugh and smile, and the more she thought about it, the more she laughed.

Luke was surprised to see his wife react in this manner. He couldn't understand why she was laughing for Ethan was an impeccable lawyer, and he aimed to bring down Compassion House. Luke attempted to refocus his wife. "I've called a few attorneys in town, and I really like one of them. His name is Aaron Wright. He's exceptional, and I think we should hire him." He was concerned when Mary continued to just laugh and smile.

"The devil is a loser; the battle is already won. 'The Lord will fight for you, and you shall hold your peace,'" Mary said, quoting Exodus 14:14. "Luke, God is going to fight for us." She sounded confident, but Luke was still concerned. He wanted to ensure they did everything they could to help God fight for them.

"I'll call Tom and see if Mr. David can recommend someone as a backup plan," Luke said.

Mary continued to laugh hysterically as she turned on praise music and began to dance before the Lord with all her might for two minutes straight.

After she finished and rested, she said to her husband, "Let's go to the movies, babe. I feel like a matinée, but first, round two of what we started last night."

Luke laughed, and danced with his wife into the bedroom, rekindling the flames that had burned the night before.

***

Mary returned to work on Wednesday, Thursday, and Friday, serving those who were emotionally and physically wounded. She ministered the hope and glory of Christ to the women. The blood of Yeshua offered to cleanse them from all unrighteousness and heal their souls and bodies. His grace was abundant enough to overshadow their shame. Those who received His Word were healed and freed; those who refused remained in darkness.

Every day after work, Mary told Luke that she wanted babies because she saw the joy that children brought, and even though they were not in the so-called prime reproducing years as they were both already in their forties, Mary still desired them. When Luke retorted, Mary quoted Psalm 127:3, "Behold, children are a heritage from the Lord, The fruit of the womb is a reward."

CHAPTER 9

The more she talked about it, the more he realized what she desired was nonnegotiable. He decided to shift his focus to wanting a son so his family name could live on.

The couple prayed to God every night for twins, a boy and a girl. Mary made sure to continuously remind Luke that when she was ovulating, they would have sex until she conceived.

When Mary saw Luke's tired expression, she made him laugh by saying, "We can't pray every night and ask God to meet our needs while failing to do our part, even if it is only for a handful of days each month. Have you not read chapter 2 in the Book of James? 'Faith without works is dead.'"

For the next week, they both went to work. Mary enrolled women who had been raped, addicted, and homeless. Luke administered treatment and procedures for his patients. At the end of the day, he knew where he would be and what he would be doing.

Friday arrived, and Luke and Mary stood together in court to face the charges of their accusers. Everyone in attendance sat down at the judge's request. To the left of her sat her opposition with their high-powered attorney, Ethan Grant, emboldened by the spirit of the Antichrist. Aaron Wright, Mary's lawyer, sat on the right, ready to refute any argument.

With the court in session, Mr. Grant spoke first, claiming that Mary had been provoking the women for several weeks and that her aggression in this altercation caused three women to seek medical attention. Following the incident, he leveled false accusations against Mary and Compassion House, claiming that the staff was untrained, abusive, and created a hostile environment.

"The church and any other entity involved in the salvation of humanity through Christ should be removed." Mr. Grant's loud voice carried easily throughout the courtroom. "Why would the city grant Mrs. Phillips a license to operate a facility like this? People should not seek religion or a savior for their mental, emotional, or physical abuse. This facility should be run by the government through state legislation."

Some of the jury as well as those seated in the courtroom nodded in agreement with Mr. Grant as he continued to degrade and accuse Mary and Compassion House staff of lacking the necessary credentials to operate a social services sector. He walked to his desk and held up a few pieces of paper.

"Your honor, I have the medical reports for the victims who were attacked by Mrs. Phillips. The victims can show further evidence of their injuries." Mr. Grant nodded to the "battered" women as they whimpered while exaggeratedly showing their arms in slings and their bruises to the judge, expecting a guilty verdict for the damages allegedly caused by Mary.

"My sincere hope is that the court considers permanently putting Compassion House out of business. Nothing further, your honor." Mr. Grant rested his case and returned to his seat. Once seated, he looked smugly over at Mary as he believed he had won and only waited to see how she would attempt to defend herself.

Luke was concerned with how eloquently the opposing lawyer stated his client's case. Not only was he seeking punitive damages, but he was alarmed to see many in the courtroom clap and appalled the antichrist agenda questioning their very right to exist. He tapped his foot and shook his leg, distressed by the crowd and the judge's blank stare as he scribbled down every-thing Mr. Grant had said.

Mary, however, was not stressed, but rather calm and assured. The joy of God gave her a peace that her adversaries in the court envied as she smiled the entire time.

When Mr. Wright stood to plead her case, God opened Mary's eyes in the Spirit. She saw an angel on the right side of the earthly judge, his big right hand on the judge's right shoulder. He was eight feet tall and didn't have wings.

CHAPTER 9

Mary was taken aback when she saw the beautiful angel, but after he smiled at her, she regained her composure. She looked around the courtroom to see if anyone else could see him, but no one else showed any sign that they could.

The righteous Judge, the just God, the God who does not change had sent him. The angel was clothed in linen, his waist girded with gold, his face like lightening, his eyes like torches of fire, his arms and feet like burnished bronze. He did not speak at all; he only smiled at Mary.

The angel lifted his left hand toward the heavens, his palm open to receive. Mary, amazed and happy to see him, asked her husband if he saw anything on the right side of the judge. Nervous and thinking she was nervous, as well, he said, "I see the judge, baby. No one else." He had no idea that the Judge of all judges had sent a ministering spirit to render verdict.

With her eyes affixed on the angel, God was assuring her victory. She would not have to fight the battle. He was there for her; the King of Kings was showing His favor.

Mr. Wright rebuked Mr. Grant's falsehoods like a skilled craftsman, analyzing each fabrication and calling on women who graduated from Compassion House to testify on behalf of the facility. They were convinced how it transformed their lives. Once lost souls, they credited Mary for being a light. Once sinking in the sin of despair and hopelessness, their feet were now established on a rock that could not be broken.

The attorney called on two more witnesses to testify about Mary and Compassion House. Both stated that if it hadn't been for Compassion Houses, they couldn't imagine where their lives would be as they confessed they had considered suicide several times.

Mr. Wright then questioned the medical diagnosis of Mary's accusers' physician. He walked to his desk, gathering information on how the physician had been sued for malpractice multiple times. With the paperwork in his hand, he read statements from seven patients claiming the physician had misdiagnosed them, causing more complications than when they came to him.

He presented the paperwork to the judge, who read it thoroughly. When the judge asked Mr. Grant if he wanted to refute the evidence, he replied, "No, your honor."

Mr. Wright then proceeded to call Mary's accusers' credibility into question by displaying a history of slip and fall "accidents" in supermarkets as well as car "accidents." Each time, the women sued by claiming an injury, but when evaluated by a physician, the physician found no injuries related to their claims after reading the medical reports, and the attorney presented the evidence to the judge.

With the judge overlooking the evidence, he asked the opposition if he wanted to rebut this information. "No, your honor, I would not," Mr. Grant snapped as he shook his head, knowing that his case was doomed.

Luke tightened his grip on his wife's hand, excited as he saw victory on the horizon, but Mary continued to smile while looking at the angel who smiled at her with a beautiful bright smile. Her husband whispered in her ear, "We are going to win, baby," but Mary did not turn to face him, nor did she flinch. She kept her eyes on the angel who was rendering the verdict in her favor.

With his final statement, Mr. Wright asked all who worked at Compassion House to stand. The angel raised his left hand as they rose to their feet. Twelve witnesses stood up in unison. The angel smiled all the more as did Mary, both of them not taking their eyes off of one another. The judge allowed some of the staffers to speak. Much to the displeasure of the opposing attorney, they echoed the sentiments of the witnesses before them. They spoke highly of Mary and Compassion House and said the Lord was using this institution to save, restore, and prosper women entrusted in their care.

Hearing enough testimonies from the witnesses and disproving the allegations of the accusers the judge was ready to render his verdict.

CHAPTER 9

"I find the defendant Mary Phillips not guilty. Compassion House will remain open with Mrs. Phillips continuing operations as its owner. This court is adjourned."

When the earthly judge delivered his verdict, the angel on his right vanished. Supporters of Mary and Compassion House erupted in applause.

Luke jumped to his feet, kissed his wife, who was still smiling, and congratulated her. As she walked out of the courtroom triumphant, she looked back, hoping to see the angel one more time, but he was gone. The scripture Isaiah 33:22 came to her mind. *For the Lord is our Judge, our Provider, and our King, and He will save us.*

God had saved Mary. He had saved Compassion House and her people. He had fought for her and victory now belonged to the King! Mary invited everyone who stood for and testified on her behalf back to her home. She thanked them for their support and catered a feast to celebrate their victory. She raised her glass and toasted her God, quoting Psalm 75:7. "'But God is the Judge: He puts down one, and exalts another.'" That Friday night and throughout the weekend, the people feasted and celebrated the Judge for being just and true.

Monday, Mary sat down with the marketing and public relation departments of Compassion House to spread the news that they had been victorious. The teams devised slogans, statements, and headlines controlling the narrative and shedding the light on all the good that Compassion House had done, was doing, and would continue to do in the future.

They called and posted statements demanding apologies from all local and some national television stations. Those who were decent and conscience verbalized their apologies, while some posted apologies to Mary and Compassion House on their social media platforms.

Throughout the rest of the week, Mary received enormous feedback from the community. People who knew her story came from all over to interview her. For months, Mary was the face of Compassion House, appearing in interviews with secular and religious magazines as well as television shows and radio stations.

God was shining His light on His daughter, and people came from all over the world to see what God was doing. Every time Mary entered a room, she was greeted with cheers and claps. She was loved and adored for her story and for founding Compassion House.

Instead of shaming her, journalists and reporters rewrote their stories to praise her. When they looked back at her history, they didn't talk about her failures and shortcomings, but about her God's grace. They wrote how Mary had triumphed over all odds and how her God had lifted her head.

With all of the news clippings going viral and trending, the favorable publicity compelled people to donate to Compassion House. When they heard the testimonies and saw lives transformed, people opened their hands in generosity, even those who did not call Yeshua Lord gave out of their hearts. The finance department reported daily giving's over one thousand percent. Some weeks, millions of dollars were received.

Compassion House flourished! Mary's enemies and those who possessed the spirit of the Antichrist fled. In trying to shame her, they elevated her. In trying to close her down, they opened her up grandly and she became renowned.

People ran to her instead of fleeing. She could now see the God of Genesis 50:20. *But as for you, you meant evil against me; but God meant it for good, in order to bring about as it is this day, to save many alive.*

With prosperity and demand, Compassion House built a second location in Arizona and it was filled to capacity in a week. Women who were reborn and successfully passed Compassion House curriculum were hired at the facility. They went to accredited schools and learned to be counselors, therapists, and psychologists. All were well equipped to minister to the hurt, oppressed, and violated.

CHAPTER 9

Mary began to write books and give speeches all over the world. The more she told her story, the more grace clothed her; wherever she went, she preached God's grace and mercy. She spoke boldly about no matter how low one falls, how filthy their sins have stained them, or how dirty their rags may be, they could be cleaned by washing in the blood of the Lamb!

Her message was affixed and affirmed in Matthew 22:12 as God invited all of His kingdom to His wedding feast. *So he said to him, 'Friend, how did you come in here without a wedding garment?' and his was speechless.*

Mary told her audience that they were invited to this great feast, but that they must change their garments. She told them that the enemy would never be able to defeat her God! She witnessed that he would never be able to out do the King of Kings and the Lord of Lords.

She shouted to all, "Where sin abounded, grace abounded much more!" People with a heart to repent heard the word and came to the Savior.

She preached the God of love, compassion, and mercy. She knew Him and she shouted His Word in Hebrews 8:12. "'For I will be merciful to their unrighteousness, and their sins and their lawless deeds I will remember no more!'"

Mary and Compassion House were doing what no city, state, or country could do. She introduced women who were wounded and cast down to the One who could really heal them and lift them out of the miry clay. The little girl from Baxley, Georgia grew and grew. The more her feet tread, the more she gained dominion. Compassion House increased to include locations in Nevada, Utah, Wyoming, North and South Dakota, until eventually, every state in America had a facility.

The blessings of the Lord poured so heavily upon His daughter and the works of her hands that the windows of heaven opened up internationally. The first country that asked for a Compassion House in was Canada, then Argentina. Brazil was next, followed by countries in Africa and then Asia began to call for their services.

CHANGING FILTHY GARMENTS

Quilla Mae had been correct in her prophecy she had bared witness to over twenty years ago. God's prophet, Joshua Reuben, was indeed a true prophet of God. He had made her a blessing to the nations the God of Abraham, Isaac, and Jacob used her to heal many, and her name was known throughout the earth.

When life seemed as if it could not get any better, God blessed her even more. While speaking in Dublin, Ireland opening another Compassion House, she felt ill and thought it was food poisoning, so she retired early to her hotel room hoping to sleep it off. She took medication hoping that it would settle her stomach and ease the pain, but it did not.

A small bubble of hope grew within her when she realized what could be "wrong" with her. The next morning, she went to the convenience store next door and purchased a pregnancy test. She waited impatiently until she finally two little lines appear on her test. Looking to the key on what the result meant, she couldn't help but scream with joy. She was pregnant!

When she arrived at the airport, Luke was waiting with the car in the arrival line. She couldn't wait until they got home; she had to tell him right away! Pulling the pregnancy test from her purse, she happily showed it to him and told him that he was going to be a father.

They praised God loudly and cried tears of joy, she had finally conceived! People honked their horns in frustration, but the Phillips were unconcerned. The soon-to-be father screamed out for the entire world to hear, "I'm going to be a father!" When the impatient people heard, they honked their horns turned from frustration to approval, happy for the soon-to-be parents.

They went home and celebrated, telling all of Mary's friends and family. Mary canceled many of her speaking engagements and Compassion House openings in order to focus on having a healthy pregnancy and baby. When they went to their doctor for the gender reveal, they were given yet another surprise.

"There is not one, but two babies in there," Doctor Denise said.

CHAPTER 9

Luke, surprised, immediately inquired, "Are you certain?"

"Yes, Mr. Phillips. I'm sure I can see a penis and a vagina clearly. Have a look."

They looked, and it was so. Yahweh had answered their prayer, the many prayers and alms had come up to Him as a memorial, and He remembered their effective prayer. They praised the King in front of their doctor in her office, unafraid of what the other faculty staffers thought or said.

Months later, Mary gave birth to a boy named Nehemiah and a girl named Naomi. She spent the majority of her time raising her children and used her free time to focus more on her writing. Though she did speak at events, it was never at the same frequency as before. She remained in Los Angeles, working out of the first ever Compassion House.

When she wasn't in California, she spent time at the ranch she had purchased next door to Quilla Mae's ranch. Luke sold his practice and volunteered with Doctors Without Borders.

Quilla Mae continued to teach Sunday school; she adored children and would frequently bring her entire class to the ranch to ride horses, play tennis, and study the Lord's Word. Prophet Joshua continued to prophesy what the Lord had commanded him to and traveled around the world teaching, edifying, and prophesying to God's people.

Mary never sinned again. Her hands remained clean and her heart remained pure, just as God did for Joshua in Zechariah 3:3-4.

Now Joshua was clothed with filthy garments, and was standing before the Angel. Then He answered and spoke to those who stood before Him, saying, "Take away the filthy garments from him." And to him He said. "See, I have removed your iniquity from you, and I will clothe you with rich robes."

Lightning Source UK Ltd.
Milton Keynes UK
UKHW050706060223
416538UK00012B/665